A. B.

Savillon's Elegies, or Poems

A. B.

Savillon's Elegies, or Poems

ISBN/EAN: 9783744716390

Printed in Europe, USA, Canada, Australia, Japan

Cover: Foto ©Andreas Hilbeck / pixelio.de

More available books at **www.hansebooks.com**

FRONTISPIECE.

View of Harrow School

J. Cruikshanks Del.   Author Inv.   B. Reading Sculp.

O say then whence proceeds the deep-fetch'd sigh,
That tear which gushes from the pensive eye?
Or why with chearless step thus steal along
To bid farewell amid the anxious throng? —

SAVILLON's ELEGIES,

OR,

POEMS,

WRITTEN BY

A GENTLEMAN, A. B.

LATE OF THE UNIVERSITY OF CAMBRIDGE.

*" Qui fit, Mæcenas, ut nemo, quam fibi fortem,
feu ratio dederit, feu fors objecerit, illâ
Contentus vivat : laudet diverfâ fequentes ?"*

HORACE, *Liber Primus, Satyra I.*

London:

PRINTED BY T. RICKABY,

FOR HOOKHAM AND CARPENTER,

NEW BOND-STREET.

1795.

INTRODUCTION.

MOST of the following Poems have appeared in our different Journals, under the fignatures of J. W. SOLANDER, NOX, &c. The principal object of arranging them in their prefent form, is to gratify the wifhes of particular friends, and I lament on this account, that many of my juvenile performances, (and among them fome of thofe which I prized the moft) are loft or deftroyed; fuch, however, as I have been able to collect, are here intruded to their notice.—Written at a period, ere tafte had refined, or judgment fufficiently ripened the underftanding, they were never intended to brave the Critic's rod, nor to vie for the mead of praife, and their beauties (if they poffefs any) confift more in the penfive language of fentiment, than in the rapid and fome-times unintelligible flight of fuperior genius to the Parnaffian Mount.

A perfon who writes at thirty, and revifes his work at fifty, may have many improvements to add; and it will not be expected by the candid reader, that the poetic effufions of one, who has not reached the former period of life, fhould equal in brilliancy the productions of thofe who have had longer experience

to embellifh, and fan into fire, the firft fparks of
their native genius.—The majority of thefe Effays
were penned, ere I had fcarce attained the age of
manhood, being compofed during the interval of
my entrance at, and my quitting the Univerfity,
when, during the vacations, at a diftance from my
affociates, and in the receffes of a beloved retreat,
I touched the firft chords of my melancholy lyre.—
In looking over the priftine efforts of my humble
Mufe, by the aid of the pruning knife, I might, perhaps, have rendered them more worthy the attention
of thofe who honor them with their patronage, but
as they were never the lucubrations of deep ftudy,
with little confideration, I refolved not (in this refpect, however) to amend the errors, or polifh the
ideas of my early youth, but to prefent them in the
fame fimple garb in which they originally met the
public eye.

Thofe lines and ideas which I was confcious, or
even fufpected, were not my own, are diftinguifhed
with quotation marks: if, therefore, I have innocently involved myfelf in the guilt of plagiarifm, the
offence, it is prefumed, will not be deemed paft re-
demption: the Bard who founds the fame tragic
lyre with his neighbour, will fometimes catch a note,
and fet it to mufic as his own, without any intention
to deceive.

It is a misfortune with many in the very early part of life to abuſe nature, by forming too mean an opinion of their own faculties :— the diffident ſtripling hangs down his head in ſhame, and endeavours to evade the queſtion of experience; while the *forward* youth, endowed with more confidence, but poſſibly inferior talents, boldly ſtrikes into the track of information, and challenges inquiry; he hears the voice of applauſe thunder in his ears, and carries off the palm of genius, which by natural right, is not unfrequently the property of the other: the former may be compared to the baſhful roſe, which, (though of ſuperior beauty perhaps, but unconſcious of its bluſhing powers) appears to droop beneath the pride of the gaudy tulip, propt up againſt the frowning tempeſt; and the timid mind, like the tender plant, requires to be defended againſt the north wind; the ſlighteſt injury will depreſs the ſpirits of ſome, though naturally courageous, while others, awake to wrongs, but of leſs delicate feelings, will ſoar above the threats of malice, and diſperſe into air the breath of unmerited calumny: we look up to a great genius with an eye of admiration, but I am not ſure if I would wiſh to be that man, becauſe I think the perſon of moderate capacity *happieſt* of the two; he ſteers his little bark through a leſs troubled ſea, and avoids ſplitting upon the rocks of envy.

Devoted, when only five years old, to combat the troubles of a public school, numbering at that time, (I believe) upwards of three hundred boys, I had many a storm to weather, and many a buffet to conquer: running from the confined illiterate nursery into a learned extensive seminary, where the pupils have generally imbibed their first rudiments at lesser schools, my little spirit, unable to brook the mortification of ignorance, laboured under the pressure of ideal inferiority, and from the supposition of its being impossible to rival my class-mate of superior years and learning, I was discouraged from trying the extent of those abilities, (however trivial they might be) with which Nature had gifted me; but time gradually draws aside the veil of self-modesty, and emancipates us from error. As I encreased in years, I confess, I grew up in indolence, and my cotemporaries, with whom I was in habits of intimacy, will bear witness to the pastimes of a truant-boy, throwing aside his theme for the rustic sports of a village fair, and of a college youth, enabled to mix in the circle of gaiety and pleasure, consigning Euclid to his dungeon, for the more easy and fashionable instructions of a Newmarket Jockey:—More ambitious to gain the *love* of my companions, than the approbation of my master, I endeavoured to excel in *gymnastic* exercises; I was a hero of the bat and ball, and few perhaps furpaffed me at leap-frog, in trundling the hoop, or at the top-race; but I followed not with equal courage and agility, the martial Homer through the field of battle:— the lag hound, though often as fleet as many others in the pack, muft be whipped up to his duty; but the confequences which followed a difobedience to the fummons of the morning bell, were not fufficiently terrific to roufe me from the arms of Morpheus; and this idle habit involved me in many difficulties: but however fevere our fufferings may have been, we caft back a grateful eye towards the fpot where our early friendfhips were formed; where the fons of Nobility and Traffic went hand in hand; and the generous mind cherifhes a reverential love for thofe inftructors, who have been our firft guides in the paths of knowledge and of truth.—Ye dear haunts, within the bounds of Harrow, of my thoughtlefs, boyifh days, thy objects live in fond remembrance, and reflect many a frolic fcene, and many a happy hour!— I afk pardon of my ftrange readers, (if any fuch there be) fhould thefe obfervations be deemed a digreffion from the fubject, but in introducing them to the contents of the following pages, the author thought it not unneceffary to give fome little defcription of himfelf, and of the country which gave birth to his folitary Mufe.

An unpoſſeſſed ſomething is ever ſought after to
render more proſperous the ſtate of man: In youth
we look forward to pleaſures engendering in the womb
of time, Hope ſports before our eyes, and prolific
Fancy paints the ſmiling plain of Futurity, ſtrewed
with roſes ; and the inexperienced mind receives
ſuch delight in travelling through theſe deluſive regions, that, careleſs of thoſe bleſſings at our command, we ſuffer the preſent moments to paſs unen-
joyed away, looking forward to ſome more diſtant
view ; where the fabric is erecting, which is to contain our every deſire,— the Paradiſe within, whoſe
envied limits meanders the ſoft ſtream of uninter-
rupted happineſs: but, alas! the meſſenger of *Truth*,
with thoſe glad tidings which are to complete our
wiſhes, ſtill remains at an imaginary diſtance, and
day after day, elapſes in vain, to convince us of our
folly: from theſe reflections, in a great meaſure, may
have iſſued the Author's mournful ſong; naturally
of a deſponding (though I hope an eaſy) temper,
I too early imbibed ſentiments, which tinctured my
mind with a kind of romantic ſadneſs, and I took up
MELPOMENE's doleful pipe to encourage and to in-
dulge it.—To me it was a pleaſing taſk, to traverſe
alone the ſhady ſolitude, where the peaceful nightingale poured forth her ſong; or at ſilent eve to wan-
der to the mouldering abbey, and as the bird of night

repeated to the moon his difmal ftrain, to meditate the tale of woe : and which, though frequently originating in fiction, may too often be verified, were we to trace out the fecret abode of mifery;— for how often might we difcern the wretched *Captive*, lingering upon his bed of ftraw; the ruined *Orphan*, in tears of anguifh, recalling to memory the paft feafon of her innocence: and the diftracted *Lover*, raving over the manes of his departed JULIA! It would be difparaging the gifts of Providence and of Nature, were I to infinuate, that my forrows flowed from the fource of cruel *felf*-misfortune; in the early fpring of life, with a fair profpect before me, I had reafon to be content and happy; but where is the Being;— the fage Philofopher, who can juftly claim the epithet of *happy?* There exifts an intermediate fpace between what we term happinefs and the gulph of mifery, and I wrote not, becaufe I was myfelf *wretched*, but becaufe I felt for the wretchednefs of others.

Well aware as I am, how unacceptable would be the offerings of a weeping Mufe, to the gay and the unthinking, I am not the lefs fanguine, that thofe for whofe perufal her plaintive effufions are chiefly intended, fhould they fail in affording pleafure, will not be reprobated for the fentiments they convey. As to others, into whofe hands accident may direct them, they muft take their chance; and, however fmall may be the portion of their merit, written as they were, without the fear of cenfure, or the hope of praife, fhould they inculcate nothing to condemn, the author's endeavours will meet their expected reward.

₂ When firft thefe Poems went to prefs, they were intended only for the perufal of private friends, but from the flattering en-comiums beftowed on them by impartial Readers, added to the confideration, that the artift's talents juftly authorize an exemption from obfcurity; the author has been induced to wave his diffidence in this refpect, and by extending the number of copies, to offer them to the countenance of thofe, among the public, whofe fimple tafte may accord with his own writings.

CONTENTS.

SAVILLON's ELEGIES

AND

POEMS.

ADIEU TO HARROW.

WRITTEN ON THE AUTHOR'S LEAVING SCHOOL.

AT length the wifh'd-for day's arriv'd, that day
Which Fancy pictur'd oft in bright array;
When every thought-fwoln trouble would be o'er,
And *Greek* and *Latin* clog the brain no more;
When joys awaited, numberlefs to tell,
And fcenes where varied pleafures ever dwell.

O fay then whence proceeds the deep-fetch'd figh,
That tear which gufhes from the penfive eye?
Or why, with chearlefs ftep thus fteal along,
To bid farewell amid the anxious throng?
Oh, my dear friends, true partners of each joy,
When nought our blended pleafures could annoy;
How oft, when loos'd from Homer's tragic tale,
We've painted future blifs o'er Windred's ale. (Note A*)

* See Notes at the end.

How (when at college met) our joys we'd crown,
And fpurn the pride that fwells the filken gown;
Then vow'd in general friendfhip to unite,
Pure was the origin,—the purpofe bright;
And thou, Black Ben, who oft with threatning nod, (B)
Haft bid me wait the vengeance of the rod;
Can *you* enforce a tear? But yet it flows,
A fweet remembrancer of all my woes;
And tells me *Juftice*, with auftere command,
Directed thus my upright mafter's hand.

My Arnold, fhall I quit, unnotic'd, you, (c)
Without one thought, one kind, one laft adieu!
A tender fprig intrufted to your care,
You fcreen'd the fapling from the winter's air:
Full many a fag I 'fcap'd up Harrow hill;
By you protected from the tyrant's will;
Accept then, here, the greeting of my heart,
'Tis Cuftom's laws compel me to depart.
Adieu, fweet grove! beneath whofe fpreading fhade (D)
I oft invok'd the Mufes' friendly aid:
Oft there, with plodding gait, I've paus'd along,
When ftudy forc'd me from the playful throng:
And you, ftern lion! who with roaring voice, (E)
My flumbers broke, and made me curfe thy noife.

And now my friends,—but hark ! the calling bell,
Yet one more hearty fqueeze, and then farewell !
I go to fteer my bark on dang'rous feas,
And dread the ruffle of each flender breeze:
Yet, fill'd with thy beft cheer, in hopes I fail,
And gather ftrength againft th' impending gale:
Then fare-ye-well, tho' fure in leaving you,
To *real* happinefs I bid adieu !

THE
SCHOOL-BOY's FIRE-SIDE.

THE timid boy, releas'd from Virgil's tale,
With fault'ring ftep, and ghaftly vifage pale,
The learned threfhold quits, and bends his way
To wonted reft, yet fears his looks pourtray:
While, thro' the leaflefs trees, the wintry blaft
Now howls, and ftrikes his tim'rous foul aghaft!
With quicken'd ftep he haftes, now backward turns,
Now gath'ring courage, prefent danger fpurns!
Till reach'd the lone church-yard, his bofom heaves
The fwell, nor Fear a ray of comfort leaves:
Yet ftriving to fubdue each fancied dread,
He whiftles thro' the manfions of the dead,
Nor cafts once glance behind; now thinks he feels
Some midnight phantom grafping at his heels.
At length, each terror fled, he braves the blaft,
And fearlefs ftops, to view the horrors paft.
Then onward haftes, to tell with keen defire
His ready ftory round the winter's fire.

And now, affembled round the hearth, each boy,
With fear each bofom pants, and now with joy;
His woeful tale begins, and now he boafts,
That by the church he faw *three* white-rob'd ghofts:

Now vows he faw each iffue from its tomb ;
A virgin one refembled—in her bloom !
In bloody veft, another feem'd to tell,
That by the murderer's flaught'ring hand he fell:
A *third* appear'd, more ghaftly than the reft,
Three difmal groans re-echoed from his breaft;
A warrior's weapon in his hand he bore,
And on his head the cap of vengeance wore;
Then fwiftly glancing 'crofs his mazy fight,
Defcended to the filent realms of night.

" Now clofer crowd the throng around the blaze,"
And, fear-ftruck, view each other with amaze;
Nor dares e'en one to caft a look behind,
Left Fancy paint fome goblin to his mind.
The bluft'ring wind the time-worn roof now rends ;
Blown from its top, the broken tile defcends :
Now ftarts each comrade from his tott'ring feat—
All from the *haunted* room in hafte retreat.
The hour of reft arriv'd, each feeks his bed,
And pents beneath the clothes his reftlefs head :
In lengthen'd darknefs lingers on the night,
Swift round the bed, Fear's vifions take their flight,
'Till, from the mind, each terror gradual flies,
As glad Aurora ftreaks the dawning fkies.

THE
CHILD OF WOE.

This Poem was intended to represent the **Situation** *of a* GENTLEMAN, *whose Life had been a Series of* **unmerited Misfortunes.**

ERST into being from the womb I **glow'd**,
  Misfortune hover'd round, imperious **foe** !
Thefe eyes in bitter ftreams prophetic flow'd,
  And ufher'd into life the Child of **Woe.**

When firft **the** breaft its nurturing nipple gave,
  To force **the** milky drop **thefe** gums refus'd;
Yet doom'd by fate the ills of **life to** brave,
  " I grew **to** age, neglected, fcorn'd, abus'd."

Oh ! whence my forrows do ye conftant **flow ?**
  When will the fource be dry from whence ye fpring?
When Pity on this wretch her calm beftow ;
  Oh ! when this breaft will mifery ceafe to fting ?

When penfive from my bed each morn I rife,
  And caft my tearful eyes the fcene around;
The Sun, alas ! his chearing beam denies,
  For *me* no ray of comfort there is found.

But round this cottage drear, perpetual night
   O'er day's bright orb her gloomy mantle fpreads;
Oft here the fcreech-owl wings his dufky flight,
   And o'er my roof his plaintive mourning fheds.

The wretch that pines within the prifon-gate,
   Proves not the torture of my foul's diftrefs ;
Ah! happier far than mine, his deftin'd fate,
   Tho' guilty chains his fetter'd limbs opprefs.

But, prov'd this breaft fome interval from pain,
   Or heav'd the figh opprefs'd with *common* grief;
I'd ceafe to fpeak my woes, nor e'er complain,
   Or pray to diftant pity for relief.

Content I'd brood in filence o'er my lot,
   And fhare, compos'd, the ills bequeath'd mankind;
" But when by parent and by friend forgot,"
   Then hard's the tafk to foothe the troubled mind.

Hear me, thou Monarch of all-ruling might,
   And pour down mercy on a wretch's head ;
Clofe faft thefe eyes in never-waking night,
   And deign my wearied foul in Heav'n a bed.

Yet ſtop, nor let me daring vent aloud
  My ſorrows thus, nor heedleſs curſe my doom;
An angel Fancy paints in yonder cloud,
  That whiſpers peace, woe dies within the tomb.

Reſign'd, then ſuffer patiently thy pain,
  Nor cenſure thus thy mighty Maker's will;
With duteous awe thy preſent ills ſuſtain,
  And ſoon eternal peace thy woes ſhall ſtill.

Rend then, Adverſity, this care-worn breaſt,
  "Deep let me drain the cup of bitter grief;"
'Till, fill'd my inſatiate ſoul, it flies to reſt,
  And finds in Heav'ns bleſt realms its due relief.

ODE TO RETIREMENT.

O, LEAD me to fome hermit's fhelter'd cell,
　Or find my fteps fome peafant's homely cot,
Where genuine peace and fweet contentment dwell,
　Where riches vanifh, and where pride's forgot.

Where no ftern porter ope's the folding door,
　Re-echoing forth its haughty mafter's wealth ;
And breathes denial to the friendlefs poor,
　My Lord's from home, or, *not in perfect health.*

Where no ambition fires the fwelling breaft,
　No courtly fop array'd in garb moft grand ;
Nor fplendid chariot fhews the baron's creft,
　Nor glift'ning pannel apes the bloody hand.

Hence, all ye gaudy trappings of parade !
　Ye grated lattices, ye coftly domes !
I value not your charms, nor court your aid,
　Ye taftelefs joys, where pleafure rarely comes.

Grant me, ye Gods ! Retirement's rural blifs,
   Beyond the grafp of Riches' potent fway ;
Where no vile art beguiles the maiden's kifs,
   Nor gorgeous title ftamps the bridal day.

Where Falfehood's fulfome tale no longer apes
   The mafk of Truth, in Flatt'ry's borrow'd guile ;
Nor high-fwoln Pride at gilded Honor gapes,
   Nor fordid Intereft courts the great man's fmile.

Here, fhelter'd in the valley's fweet retreat,
   Each rifing morn with happinefs I'll crown ;
Here will I fix (my guefts) the Mufe's feat,
   And fpurn with them the follies of the town.

At dawn of light I'll tend the fky-lark's note,
   That twitters gaily o'er my ftraw-topp'd fhed ;
And as he tunes to blifs his chanting throat,
   I'll fing 'till from my humble roof he's fled.

When Phœbus bright here beams his fcorching rays,
   I'll fit beneath this oak, that fhades the dale ;
Or, wand'ring thro' the wood's intricate ways,
   I'll court the zephyrs of the fanning gale.

At filent eve I'll feek the peaceful grove,
 The murm'ring brook that gently glides along;
Or, fhould to village fports my foot-fteps rove,
 I'll join in ruftic dance the thoughtlefs throng.

Here will I fhare of mirth the welcome meal,
 No pride, dread foe to blifs, fhall fting my breaft,
When fill'd with pleafure, from the board I'll fteal,
 And homeward plod my way to downy reft.

There, free from care, I'll lull my foul to fleep,
 In pleafing dreams the nightly hours fhall fly;
No lordly frown fhall caufe thefe eyes to weep,
 Nor ftern ambition bid this breaft to figh.

Begone, thou deftin'd foe to earthly blifs!
 Too long you've tenanted this unpaid breaft;
Fly far my roof, replete with happinefs,
 And let Humility its inmate reft.

Away all greatnefs and thy glittering train,
 Seek not to dim thefe eyes with pompous glare;
Nor bend thy fteps tow'rds this retir'd domain,
 For nought of thee fhall cloy my humble fare.

No titled equipage ſhall e'er be ſeen,
   To roll in paſſing grandeur o'er this plain;
No lordly gueſt, pourtray'd in graceful mien,
   Shall enter here, nor Pride a welcome gain.

But here the wearied traveller ſhall find
   A friendly hoſt, and reſt in ſoft repoſe ;
Here ſhall the wounded Soldier call to mind
   His injur'd worth, nor tell unheard his woes.

Here ſhall my ſoul, content, true pleaſure prove,
   Nor longer flit on Fortune's doubtful wing;
Hence, ſhall its flight on haſty pinions move,
   Tow'rds that retreat, where ſorrows ceaſe to ſting.

O, come then, Happineſs ! be thou my gueſt,
   Sweet flow'rets round my cottage daily ſtrew ;
'Till Heav'n in pity grants my ſole requeſt,
   And thither call'd, I'm join'd in peace with you.

THE CAPTIVE.

HAIL, happy morn! how charming are thy rays
   To minds at eafe, from dire oppreffion free;
No chearly beam, alas! *my* grief allays,
   Depriv'd of life's chief fweetner—Liberty.

Thou rifing fun that fpread'ft around delight,
   To thefe fad drooping eyes thou fhin'ft in vain;
Thy powers are loft on me, tho' e'er fo bright,
   Thou canft not loofe thefe chains, or eafe my pain.

With thee the ready ploughman quits his bed,
   Purfues, fecure from care, his daily toil;
With thee retires, refeeks his humble fhed,
   Thoughtlefs what fate awaits the morrow's broil.

How happy he! how calmly pafs his days!
   His fole ambition refts in Liberty!
Dear name! on thee, alas! in vain I gaze,
   Sentenc'd for life to dire captivity.

On me each wiſtful morn freſh ſorrow ſheds,
 Each night creates new horrors in my breaſt ;
Dread night ! that o'er my cell grim Darkneſs ſpreads,
 And ſpurns me from the lulling arms of Reſt.

Oh ! balmy ſleep, that rid'ſt the ſoul of care,
 In vain I 'nvoke thee to my bed of ſtraw;
Thou ſpurn'ſt the wretched Captive's humble fare,
 And bidſt him reap the fruits of cruel war.

In this drear cell nought elſe but Sorrow reigns,
 The ſole companion of each hapleſs hour ;
Save when at night the lonely owl complains,
 In diſmal note from yonder ruin'd tow'r.

Save when by Cynthia's pallid dawn I view
 The tiger, ſtealing o'er the diſtant waſte ;
Save when the rav'nous wolf, with hideous hue,
 Purſues his deſtin'd prey in eager haſte.

Save when the ſhip-wreck'd mariner I view,
 Imploring mercy from the hoſtile wave ;
In vain he calls, now ſhrieks the frantic crew,
 Employ'd each hand the freighted bark to ſave.

Now rolls the threat'ning thunder o'er their heads,
 Now Boreas with redoubled vengeance blows;
Each billow now the feeble veffel dreads,
 'Till vanquifh'd quite, fhe yields to conq'ring foes.

Now plung'd in ftormy Neptune's craggy deep,
 Th' intrepid feaman feeks his wat'ry grave;
'Till rock'd at length into eternal fleep,
 He refts companion of the murm'ring wave.

Yet, envious fate, bereft of every care,
 Through bufy life the dreary voyage is o'er;
The dreaded port is made, where wan Defpair
 The faithlefs breaft of man molefts no more.

Where ftern Ambition ends her vain career,
 Where Pride no more in ftately grandeur reigns;
Where mighty Kings, with peafants fhare their cheer,
 And where the Captive, Liberty regains.

Ye Gods, who rule above, then hear my prayer,
 Releafe my limbs from this dire load of pain;
Then free'd I'll bid defiance to each care,
 And drown my forrows in yon boift'rous main.

Yet vain the wifh! my forrows nought avail,
   No feeling ear will liften to my woes;
Nor yet will pitying eye, nor profperous gale,
   Once lend their aid to vanquifh thefe dread foes.

Then doom'd, alas! to linger out my days,
   In thefe drear realms my forrows ne'er will ceafe;
'Till Time at length my ev'ry grief allays,
   And locks me in the arms of lafting Peace.

LOUISA,

AN ELEGY;

WRITTEN

UPON A LADY, WHO PERISHED ON HER VOYAGE TO INDIA,

Whither she had followed a YOUNG MAN, *mutually attached, in consequence of a Matrimonial Engagement.*

THE full-orb'd moon in solemn splendor shone,
 And deck'd in silv'ry garb the still-hush'd wave;
The weary winds had ceas'd their plaintive moan,
 When sad I sought Louisa's wat'ry grave.

No sound was heard—dead silence reign'd around,
 Invoking sadness to the awful scene;
The drowsy flocks lay hush'd within their mound,
 And thoughtless sped the shepherd o'er the green.

'Twas then, distracted, on the sea-lav'd shore,
 I chid in frantic grief th' insatiate main;
That lost Louisa's image did restore,
 And told the secret troubles of my brain.

Ah, fweet Louife! accurs'd, yet dear the day,
  That dropp'd thee from thy Mother-Angel's cloud;
Too foon thus mingled with the mould'ring clay,
  Too foon enwrapt in Death's refiftlefs fhroud.

She, who was wont to raife the forrowing head,
  When funk beneath the pillow of defpair;
Oft haplefs there with winged fpeed fhe fled,
  And minifter'd relief with anxious care.

Yea, fhe was gentle as the twilight dove,
  Untaught by Art, in Vice's path unknown;
Her heart was form'd to innocence and love,
  The Child of Virtue, and the Grace's own.

Her form was elegance in native eafe,
  Her face excell'd the pencil's utmoft art;
What fenfe could fpurn fuch beauty, made to pleafe?--
  What breaft of fteel refift the fatal dart?

Then tell me, rueful billow, is fhe rock'd
  To endlefs fleep beneath thy furging foam?
Or does her fpirit, 'till in peace it's lock'd
  With Henry's foul, a wretched wand'rer roam?

Yet, fure fuch worth t' immortal blifs has fled,
  To bleffed regions of eternal peace ;
And Sifter-Angels guard her fainted bed,
  'Till Henry there his forrows fhall appeafe.

Then hafte away ! fly fwift ye ling'ring days !
  Ye weary nights in wafting forrow pafs'd ;
'Till rous'd from Death's laft fleep, I wake amaz'd
  In Heav'n ! and in Louifa's arms am clafp'd.

STANZAS

ON

HEARING THE SCREECH-OWL AT NIGHT.

I.

HARK to that plaintive voice which thrills my ears,
And wakes my tim'rous foul to midnight fears;
That vents its wailing thro' the flumb'ring air,
In founds of horror and acute defpair.

II.

'Tis the lone Screech-Owl's call! which *I* obey,
For I, like him, make gloomy night the day;
Condemn'd, like him, by Cynthia's dawn to rove,
Thro' the wild mazes of intricate love.

III.

Yes, mournful bird, to thee I fly for reft,
To woo fweet *Melancholy* to my breaft;
For in thy forrow-founding note I find
A precious balm, that foothes my frantic mind.

With thee I scale the antique ruin'd tow'r,
Or haunt the lone retreat of Cupids bow'r;
And as you vent aloud repeated woes,
In untold grief the silent tear-drop flows.

IV.

With thee I fcale the antique ruin'd tow'r,
Or haunt the lone retreat of Cupid's bow'r;
And as you vent aloud repeated woes,
In untold grief the filent tear-drop flows.

V.

When morning's tints the pale-fac'd night difpel,
You feek the hermit's roof, and *I* his cell;
Till Luna reigns again—thy call I tend,
And hail thee as my gueft and only friend.

ELEGY

ON

A FAVOURITE DOG,

Intrusted by an intimate FRIEND, *to the Care of the* AUTHOR, *during the Absence of its* MASTER, *and which was afterwards presented to him as a Token of Regard; whose death was occasioned from having received a Bite from a* MAD DOG.

ASSIST me spirits! whilst to Vixen's grave,
  With solitary step I mournful stray;
Whilst with a tear the rueful spot I lave,
  Where injur'd innocence and friendship lay.

Accurs'd the hand! and hard the savage heart!
  That drove the deadly weapon 'gainst her breast;
That breast, which ne'er till then had thought to smart,
  Beneath the hand it often had caress'd.

My friend! when thus thy Fav'rite's fate you hear,
  Intrusted late beneath Protection's wing;
How will the tiding rend your woe-struck ear,
  Oh, how your heart with pity will it wring.

Yea, often as the forrowing turf I pafs,
   Where hidden refts beneath her worth reclin'd;
So oft will Mem'ry's tear re-bathe the grafs,
   So oft recall your friendfhip to my mind.

Then reft in endlefs fleep, dear honour'd fhade,
   Departed gift of concord moft fincere;
Whilft o'er your refting place a tribute's paid,
   Whilft there a weeping mafter helps your bier.

Oh, hard the tafk ! yet fweet the chofen pain,
   Which thus reiterates Affliction's dart;
Accept the tear which forrow can't reftrain,
   The farewell token of a bleeding heart.

EPITAPH TO THE ABOVE.

A moment ftop, ye thoughtlefs paffers by,
   Ye mourning tenants of yon helplefs dome !
O, drop one mindful tear, or breathe a figh,
   Thy favourite here has found a lafting home.

STANZAS

ON

A SLEEPING INFANT.

SWEET fleeping Innocent! how bleft thy ftate,
　Thus lull'd to reft within thy mother's arms:
No anxious cares thy flumbers now await,
　Nor dream of woe, thy fpotlefs breaft alarms!

Luxuriant fleep! true balm of heav'nly blifs!
　Entic'd beneath thy watchful parent's wing:
Ah! did it laft, what joy could equal this!
　What fcenes of happinefs would each day bring!

But know, dear Babe, as thus you flumb'ring lay,
　That fhort's thy fleep, and fhort's thy tranfient reign;
For foon thofe cheeks, which now in fmiles look gay,
　The cares of life will fur with many a pain.

As now thy mother clafps thy naked frame,
　Thus gently fondled in her anxious arms:
Soon will fome rude blaft thofe bleffings maim,
　Ah! foon will waft thee from thofe fleeting charms.

Yes, foon thy fated bark its courfe muft fteer,
  Thro' troubled feas, where dangers hover round ;
Where no fond parent deigns thy cries to hear,
  Nor pitying friend will tend the diftant found.

Sleep on then, Innocent, in balmy reft,
  Thus undifturb'd, enjoy thy happy reign ;
For brief's the fpace by pleafure's thus careft,
  'Twixt fhort liv'd happinefs, and frequent pain.

STANZAS

ON

A LADY'S DEPARTURE FROM ENGLAND.

COME weep with me, ye tenants of the grove !
  Ye ſtagnate rills, ye drooping willows, moan;
The queen of birds that lately deign'd to rove,
  Thro' thy enchanted bow'rs, far off is flown.

On Nature's gifted wings of airy haſte,
  'Croſs Ocean's wave it ſeeks a diſtant realm;
Nor ſtops its courſe along the mourning waſte,
  The ſpreading oak, the foliage-cladden elm.

In vain laments, in note of heart-felt woe,
  Its hapleſs partner of the weeping grove ;
The flow'rets ſweet, which verdant there did grow,
  Now droop each head, kind emblems of their love.

Sweet voice of melody ! how cheer'd the ſwain,
  Thy ſong, there wand'ring to relate his love ;
With them, alas ! now join'd in penſive train,
  He weeps, in ſad diſmay, their abſent dove.

Ah ! cheerlefs bow'rs ! where now thy wonted charms,
   Sweet S—DC—P ! late, that deign'd a bleft retreat ?
Where now thy fpreading oaks ? their honor'd arms
   Encircling Virtue's and the Grace's feat.

Where now the plunder'd fhrubbery's boafted walk,
   That iffued fragrance forth in rofeate hue ?
Thy bloffoms fade, and weeds are left to ftalk,
   Where beauty once in native femblance grew.

Ah, me ! each fhrub now clad in deep array,
   Bewails the morn with drops of forrowing dew ;
All joy is gone, no fun now glads the day,
   Each tenant *there* to pleafure bids adieu.

Here once this drooping lilly rear'd its head,
   Each morn frefh nurture drew from Virtue's hand ;
Here too this wither'd rofe its odors fpread, ·
   And deck'd in pillag'd grace the naked land.

Here tun'd at eve fweet Philomel her throat,
   To rhyme of love, to peerlefs accents gay ;
Here warbled thro' thefe trees the thrufh its note,
   And here too, Cupid fix'd his evening lay.

Sweet daiſied mead, that rais'd its white-fraught head,
   And beam'd forth luſtre from the radiant ſun;
Where now thy borrow'd garb ? a wat'ry bed,
   Awaits thy lay, where late each beauty ſhone.

Yea, e'en the cattle conſcious ſeem to moan,
   And ſad'ning graze along the penſive plain ;
Hear how the grief-ſtruck ſky reſounds the groan,
   Re-echoed forth in melancholy ſtrain !

Ah ! Damon blithe, that whiſtled o'er theſe plains,
   And thrill'd with accents gay the ſolemn air ;
Where now thy dormant pipe ? its dulcit ſtrains,
   Which baniſh'd hence the ſhaft of canker'd care?

Where now the voice that taught thy ruſtic lute,
   To vent its notes beneath the ſilent ſhade;
That voice which deign'd to give a tongue each mute,
   Now loſt its harmony, and fled its aid.

Begone then, ſhepherd ! hence all pleaſure flies,
   Haſte far away this now-deſerted plain;
Re-ſeek thoſe bowers which boaſt this hidden prize,
   And there, *once more*, your paradiſe regain.

Here left thro' folitude alone to rove,
 I'll court each weeping gueft,—my fate deplore;
Oft fhall the tear its lofs in torrents prove,
 Where virtue chafte, and beauty charm no more.

Here on this tree, I'll carve the precious name,
 And tell its owner's worth to future days;
Here fhall it breathe in traits of living fame,
 Still fhall T—— exift in laurell'd praife.

REPLY TO SOPHIA;

Written in the Name of a FRIEND, *in Anfwer to a* LADY, *inquiring the Caufe of his Defpair.*

O, WONDER not, SOPHIA, dear,
  Why wears this cheek the fur of care;
Why leaves its cell, this tell-tale tear,
  Or, why thefe limbs thus wafted are?
Thofe charms, which hope had once ordain'd for me,
Have doom'd this breaft to lafting mifery.

O, afk not why this bofom grieves,
  It beating pants with load of woe;
Or why the troubled figh it heaves,
  By fervent love thus taught to glow?
Perufe this burning heart thou fenfelefs fair,
And read the caufe in reeking fymbols there.

Enquire not why along the fhade,
  My footfteps paufe in penfive ftalk;
And fhun the path for lovers made,
  Where Cupids prate in wanton talk?
Know, cruel nymph, to death they plod the way,
By *you* entic'd from happinefs to ftray.

ELIZA,

AN ELEGY.

HENCE from the shady grove's alluring walk,
    The cowslip'd mead, the gentle purling rill;
Give *me* the drear church-yard alone to stalk,
    And there of sorrows let me take my fill.

For long my steps Affliction's path have trod,
    Yea, long have sought the yew-tree's gloomy shade;
And oft with sorrow have imprefs'd the sod,
    Where, lock'd in sleep, my lost ELIZA's laid.

Oft there my dismal thoughts the way have led,
    When darknefs sad has clos'd the ling'ring day;
And seated 'mid the regions of the dead,
    Have moisten'd with my tears the mould'ring clay.

There oft I've mourn'd by Cynthia's pallid dawn,
    And woo'd the tolling of the deadly bell;
When Phœbus bright has cheer'd the weeping morn,
    I've sought in wild despair some hermit's cell.

There from my eyes to banifh hateful day,
  And foothe with Sorrow's balm my haplefs lot;
" For no kind friend will this breaft's grief allay,"
  ELIZA gone ! by all the world forgot.

A fairer flower Earth's bofom never bore,
  'Till wither'd by the winter's hoary blight!
A cruel blaft the tender fibres tore—
  It droop'd its head, and funk from mortal fight.

In heav'n ELIZA, if you hold your reign,
  Look down with pity on thy EDWARD's woes;
Remember him, whom *thou* haft doom'd to pain,
  And lull his frantic foul to calm repofe.

ELEGY,

WRITTEN ON AN EVENING IN SUMMER.

SWEET peaceful eve ! with penfive filence crown'd,
 Lone ftillnefs hail ! roll on ye babbling rills—
The dufky bat fwift wings his wonted round,
 And dreary darknefs tips the diftant hills.

Departing Phœbus down the weftern fky,
 In folemn grandeur hides his ruby face;
Now to their nefts the feather'd fongfters fly,
 And gloomy night fteals on in awful pace.

Nor aught is heard ! fave ruftling thro' the trees,
 On quiv'ring pinions gently borne along;
The cooling zephyr wafts its gentle breeze,
 And bears refrefhment to the lab'ring throng.

Save now and then the fcreech-owl's plaintive cry,
 " On fome rude fragment" perch'd, or mould'ring
Save PHILOMEL's their abfent mates decry, [tow'r:
 In ftrains reproachful thro' the echoing bow'r.

Save the dull sheep-bell's drowsy tinkling sound,
    At moving periods wakes the pensive ear ;
Or watchful shepherd from the fleecy mound,
    Who, whistling homeward, tends his blithe career.

Save the brown cowboy's known expressive yell,
    The moaning cattle hooping o'er the plain ;
Or cackling goose ; or, lurkers to repel,
    The mastiff howling from the 'squire's domain.

Save the hoarse raven to the rooky bow'r,
    On footy pinions wings his croaking way;
Or bee that hums around the dewy flow'r,
    Ere fateful night decrees it to decay.

All else is still ! yet hark, yon tolling bell,
    That stirs to weightier thoughts, the trembling
View the black coffin sauntering to its cell,   [soul :
    In slow obedience to stern Death's controul.

Contain'd, perhaps, therein the virgin frame,
    Of some fair maid, a sacrifice to love;
Some warrior perhaps, of private fame,   [prove.
    Whose worth, if tried, as ELLIOT's, great might

Sunk in the void of night, now Envy dies,
  Oblivion hurls her leaden fceptre round;
Abfconded in the gulph too, Malice lies,
  Till rous'd by Morning to her art profound.

Lur'd to the lulling arms of foft repofe,
  The wearied traveller quits the dufty road;
Forgets in fleep, the foldier too, his woes,
  Or o'er the flafk throws off Misfortune's load.

All, all, fave wretched me, retire to reft,
  But *my* neglected head no pillow woo's;
A thoufand troubles torture this fad breaft,
  Which perjur'd friends, to mollify, refufe.

O, hufhful night! and thou (proud ftranger) fleep!
  That frees the life-fick mortal from defpair;
" Can ye my fenfes in oblivion fteep,
  And grant a fhort-liv'd refpite to my care?"

Oh, no! nor day, nor night, allays my grief,
  Shipwreck'd I rove along the defert fhore;
Like fome loft mariner, denied relief,
  And doom'd to mourn 'till life fhall be no more.

VERSES

ON

VISITING THE TOMB OF AN UNFORTUNATE

YOUNG LADY.

WHERE yonder yew-tree fpreads its gloomy fhade,
And the lone moon, in pallid veft array'd,
Gleams thro' the dreary haunts of filent night,
Diffufing round her meditating light;
There rudely mingled with the fleeping dead,
Belov'd LAURELLA lays her care-eas'd head;
There moulders into duft the faireft frame,
That e'er to Virtue's mead deferv'd a claim;
A fweeter bud the lovely fpring ne'er knew,
Within the garden's pale, to envious view,
She bloffom'd forth, with modeft timid air,
Beneath a watchful parent's anxious care,
In bluft'ring pride there grew, confign'd to reign,
The Queen of Beauty 'mong the bafhful train.
But, ah! difaftrous fate! by heav'ns decree,
Her guardian droop'd, and died in mifery,

And left her blooming hope, with trembling fear,
To tread the mazy world,—thro' life to fteer :—
Yet, ere fhe died, bequeath'd her laft advice,
Her darling caution'd 'gainft the lures of Vice :
Depicted to her mind the path *fhe'd* trod,
" *True to herfelf, and truer to her God.*"

But fcarce had filial love the facred truft
In tears committed to its kindred duft,
When vile Seduction laid his captious fnare—
A tempeft rofe, and fcatter'd in the air,
The faded bloffoms of the withering ftem,
Deftroy'd, and naked, ftripp'd of every gem;
No more to ufher forth in bright array,
Nor fpread its ruin'd beauties to the day.
Such was LAURELLA's fate: but Truth record
The bafe affections of her perjur'd Lord.
Torn from her native roof—unheard her cries—
The villain bore away his plunder'd prize!
He flatter'd, figh'd—in vain !—for ftill no art
Could lure from rectitude her fpotlefs heart.
Defpairing thus—the madd'ning fatal bowl,
Infus'd corruption to her guiltlefs foul.

Depriv'd of fenfe, bewilder'd in a dream—
Each thought was flown of virtue and efteem,
And yielded up to man's deftructive pow'r,
She bow'd obedience in Oppreffion's hour.

Pall'd with the feaft, the fated lover fled,
And left her fenfelefs on the tainted bed !
Haplefs fhe wak'd—abandon'd, and forlorn—
Expos'd to vice, to infamy, and fcorn;
And when returning fenfe her fate reveal'd,
Afham'd to face the world—fhe droop'd conceal'd ;
Unform'd the voice of calumny to brave,
And funk repenting to an early grave.

ELEGY

ON THE SEA COAST AT MARGATE.

OFT Margate, from thy bufy fcenes I fteal,
   To feek the defert ftrand! the bleak winds roar!
There to the waves my forrows I reveal,
   And ftalk thy penfive folitary fhore.

From the rough billow tofs'd, the fea-bird foars,
   Screaming aloft the raging ocean's foam:
Burfting the furcharg'd fky, deftruction pours—
   The fhip-boy fhrieks! ftill, ftill, I onward roam.

Borne by the gale, I hear the hopelefs cry!
Hark! the diftreffing fhot! no help is nigh:
They fink, they fink! beneath my anxious fight,
Defcending to the watery realms of night.

Mark the poor ftruggling wretch, for precious life,
Cling to the fcatter'd plank with eager ftrife!
Oh! heaven, fave him! fave him! in vain my cries!
Buried in the all-devouring wave, he dies.

Yet dauntlefs ftill, upon the wafteful fhore,
   I watch the furges mount the rocky fteep;
Breaking, I hear them clafh with frantic roar,
   And fall in vanquifh'd murmurs to the deep.

And as the fenfelefs cliffs, with unmov'd pride,
The bluft'ring wave's ejective threats deride;
So, harden'd by ftern Fate, difdainful I,
Each fruitlefs menace of the ftorm defy.

Thus, as I view the wild tremendous fea,
   In awful beauty drefs'd, amaz'd, I ftand!
Yet far more charming is the fcene to me,
   Than all the fun-bright profpects of the land.

What's then the giddy ball to my fad heart,
   Or joys that float around the midnight bowl?
Can they affliction drown,— relief impart,
   Or yield kind comfort to my gloomy foul?

Oh, no! hence then, illufions vain! no more—
Deign *me* the defert ftrand—the penfive fhore.

Yet dauntless still, upon the wasteful shore,
I watch the surges mount the rocky steep;
Breaking, I hear them clash with frantic roar,
And fall in vanquish'd murmurs to the deep.

CLEORA and the BULLFINCH.

IN June, at eve, one fatal day,
Belov'd CLEORA ſtray'd away,
　　Unmindful where to roam
The blooming maid of ſweet ſixteen,
And 'clep'd by all fair Beauty's queen,
　　She left her parent's home.

Entic'd along the flow'ry mead,
Regardleſs where the path would lead,
　　She enter'd Cupid's grove;
Where little warblers tune their throats,
To mutual Love's reſponding notes,
　　Their bliſs or pain to prove.

A Bullfinch ſad among the reſt,
With doleful pipe and heaving breaſt,
　　There fix'd its plaintive lay;
The penſive mourner ſettling by,
Engag'd CLEORA's pitying eye,
　　And thus it ſeem'd to ſay :—

Ah! once like you, angelic maid,
Reflecting not that snares were laid,
   In this alluring grove ;
" I careless rov'd its sweets among,
" And wak'd its echoes with my song,"
   'Till taught by perjur'd Love.

A faithless mate in showy vest,
By Nature's hand profusely drest,
   Here wing'd his gaudy way :
He told his artful flatt'ring tale,
Seduc'd me down the flow'ry dale,
   Ah, fatal! fatal day !

Attun'd his pipe to strains of love,
Avow'd he'd ever constant prove,
   'Till Death's eventful hour ;
And thus in fleeting joys immur'd,
Our future happiness secur'd,
   We chirp'd from flow'r to flow'r.

But soon the transient bliss was o'er,
The wand'rer sung of love no more,
   Nor prais'd my plumage gay ;
But pluck'd in Pleasure's lawless zest,
The choicest feather from my breast,
   And fled, far, far away.

As thus the haplefs warbler fung,
CLEORA's breaſt (with pity wrung)
 Heav'd many a pond'rous ſigh;
But little thought the weeping maid,
While thus in Sorrow's tears array'd,
 Her own ſad fate was nigh.

Then lifting up her tearful eyes,
Advancing quick a youth ſhe ſpies,
 With all a courtier's air;
In language ſoft— with graceful eaſe,
And ſelf-enamour'd ſure to pleaſe,
 He thus addrefs'd the fair.

Long, long, coy maid of modeſty,
This heated heart has griev'd for thee,
 Let truth my paſſion prove;
Come, let's repair to yonder ſhade,
Yon umbrage bleſt, for courtier's made,
 Nor ſcorn my tale of love.

Begone, Sir, pray, return'd the nymph,
My father lives near yonder lymph,
 Where mindful ruſhes grow;—
Thy dad's aſleep, the tempter cry'd:
She faulter'd—bluſh'd—but ſtill replied,
 I muſt not, cannot go.

If then, thou cruel, harden'd fair,
You thus refuſe to hear my pray'r,
   Thoſe eyes ſhall ſee me die;
Yon mindful lymph ſhall be my bed,
Ah, there, I'll reſt this wretched head,
   And end my miſery.

CLEORA, hapleſs, wept, and ſigh'd,
Conſenting bluſhes ſtrove to hide,
   But in Deſtruction's pow'r,
And yielded up to guilty Love,
She fell within the ſilent grove,
   The victim of an hour.

Twelve months ſhe bore a harlot's name,
The pinch of want, the ſport of ſhame,
   Her parent's home denied;
" The bud of health forſook her cheek,
" Which er'ſt could boaſt its pureſt ſtreak,"
   And thus repining died.

MORAL.

Learn hence, ye blooming virgins, and beware !
   Scorn not the warning of a faithful friend;
" Know *Ruin* lurks, where Flatt'ry lays his ſnare,"
   And ſhun CLEORA's baſe untimely end.

STANZAS

ON

THE RUINS OF THE PANTHEON.

ATTEND me, Grief! whilſt o'er yon ruin'd ſpace
   My melancholy penſive footſteps tread;
Whilſt many a veſtige ſcatter'd round I trace,
   Where fam'd Pantheon rais'd its lofty head.

How fallen Grandeur diſregarded lies !
   The fabric gone,—proud Miſchief ſtalks elate;
Heap, pil'd on heap, the ſplendid atoms riſe,
   And mock the mimic hand of idle State.

Enchanting ſcenes ! now levell'd with the ground,
   Thy pleaſing views no longer greet the eye ;
The ear no more ſhall catch ITALIA's found.—
   Thy bright allurements all extinguiſh'd lie.

Here ſoftly quaver'd from MORELLI's tongue,
   Each dulcet ſtrain, pour'd forth with potent ſway;
Here NEGRI charm'd the vocal choir among,
   And held the ſenſes captive at her lay.

On that rude fpot the flighty D'EGVILLE too,
   His agile form difplay'd with magic art;
There vaulting HILLIGSBERG would fpring to view,
   And well perform no mean allotted part.

The dancers fled—the fingers vanifh'd are,—
   The harmony of CRAMER's band is o'er;
No quaint grimaces pleafe the giggling fair,
   Where gay Attraction, humbled, fmiles no more.

Now, thro' thy rooms, prepar'd for midnight mafk,
   No fable *Domino* fhall ftalk demure;
No witty Punch affume his jocund tafk,
   Nor Quacks for vapours minifter a cure.

The footy link-boy with his torch in hand,
   And voice uncouth, no longer bawls aloud;
In throngs, no footmen lac'd, infulting ftand,
   To fneer contempt upon the paffing crowd.

Hufh'd is each noife! no found annoys the ear,
   Of haughty chairmen, calling, room there, room;
No thund'ring voice that fhakes the meek with fear,
   Proclaims the fribbling Lord, or aping Groom.

Yet weep not, Mufe, at yonder empty void,
  Where, late admir'd, the magic temple ftood;
Its grace perhaps the Power above deftroy'd,
  From care peculiar for a Nation's good.

Ye made-up groups, no more to vault in air, (F)
  Enrich'd with many a fpoil from Albion's ftore;
Your patches, rouge, pearl powder, teeth prepare,
  And quit, light-heel'd, her lavifh, plunder'd fhore.

On you no more conceited beaus fhall grin,
  Become protectors of their native land ;
Thy pliant limbs that oft applaufe would win,
  No more fhall caper from their tott'ring ftand.

Quick then, depart from this ill-fated ifle, (G)
  Ye Signioras, Signiors, all farewell;
And, as ye pafs, on Englifh folly fmile,
  But fecret keep what *fhame* would blufh to tell. (H)

Let fafhion long lament the fatal flame,
  And peace, thus gain'd, in tranquil weeds appear ;
May every voice the banifh'd race proclaim,
  And Britain, ftill Britannia's title bear.

ELEGY

ON .

The sudden Departure of a FAMILY *from a* COUNTRY-HOUSE, *where they had resided many Years.*

FAIR rose the morn, in sunny vest array'd,
    Nature sat smiling o'er the new-born day;
The glowing meads their richest gems display'd,
    Beneath the splendour of bright Phœbus' ray.

When musing, SEDLEY, 'mid thy blooming flowers, (1)
    Forgetful Pride appear'd with wand in hand; (k)
And scarce allow'd farewell, depart these bow'rs,
    The despot cried, with pompous stern command.

Compell'd away! denied one poor caress,
    Shades of my early youth! belov'd retreat;
I left thy groves, thy streams, thy dear recess,
    Of tranquil solitude the peaceful seat.

Behold yon dome, with gothic walls around!
    There late, for unassuming worth admir'd:
The generous host, with modest virtues crown'd,
    Would seek repose, from worldly cares retir'd.

There bleſt, with matchleſs conſort by his ſide,
   The bliſsful, placid hours would glide away ;
Secure of children's love, the hamlet's pride,
   Ador'd by all---the rich— the poor— the gay.

But now, alas ! ah, ſad reverſe of fate !
   Flown are its charms, and each allurement gone,
The ruſtic ſtalks in ſilence paſt the gate,
   And mourns its abſent Lord, with ſtride forlorn.

The roof-decaying owl, her boding flight,
   Prophetic ſweeps along the gloomy plain ;
In ſearch of ſome rude hole, remote from ſight,
   To fix her future ſolitary reign.

Stript of its pride, ſurvey the naked lawn !
   Where now the ſportive throng of village fame,
Which late did thy deſerted void adorn ?
   The faireſt offspring of the faireſt dame !

Aſſembled there, the prattling infant crew
   Would oft the day in harmleſs mirth employ;
There would they ſkip, their jocund pranks renew,
   Thoſe pranks of youth, which never, never cloy.

There I too, once like them, in giddy play,
   "A thoughtlefs child, would fport amid thy bow'rs:"
Uncheck'd by cares, and innocently gay,
   Regardlefs of the fleeting happy hours.

Ye flow'ry meads, where oft I've toy'd along,
   And cull'd the violet blue—the primrofe fweet,—
Where oft I've bafk'd, thy od'rous fcents among,
   My little heart with happinefs replete.

This rofe, which now exalts its mufky head,
   And rich perfumes thus fcatters in the air;
A few fhort days may view for ever dead,
   Perhaps, ere long, a weed may forrow there!

Yet fate forbid! though now another's boon,
   Unfullied may thy flow'rs, thy fweets remain;
Which cold neglect might damp, alas! too foon!
   And not a flow'r its wonted fcent retain.

Robb'd of thy guard, I fear, left fome rude tread,
   May heedlefs crufh thy tender frame's fo fair;
Who now will watch around thy evening bed,
   And mark thy progrefs with a parent's care?

Ah, fhades belov'd ! for ever loft, adieu !
    Ye woods, ye ftreams, and filent, peaceful dell ;
Forbid by harfh decree, to gaze on you,
    Scenes now, alas ! to be forgot,—farewell !

LINES

ADDRESSED TO THE

AUTHOR's BROTHER,

ON BEING APPOINTED, BY A PARTICULAR FRIEND, A WRITER
TO MADRAS.

EXULT, fond youth! proclaim thy guardian's praife,
Implore him long, long life, and prosp'rous days;
Attune thy reed, and fing to friendfhip true,
The nobleft patron of the noble few!

O had I POPE's or DRYDEN's happy lyre,
To found the merits of the generous Sire,
Who thus to Fortune's road has been thy guide;
Has fill'd thy heart with joy, thy mind with pride;
I'd roufe the *Mufes Nine*, each vale fhould ring,
In concord join'd, each bard his worth fhould fing;
Tune then thy reed, and fing to friendfhip true,
The nobleft patron of the noble few!

Blcft youth! now *Fortune* with her gaudy wings
Around thee flutters, paints a thoufand things—
Predicts the joys which pow'rful riches yield,
And all thy care is how the load to wield.

Gigs, phaetons, and nabob-chariot gay,
Before thy fancy dance in airy play :
Nor does one care thy future blifs annoy,
Rich in the thought, that pleafures never cloy ;
Thus may it prove, when wealth is in thy pow'r,
And nought occur to damp the feftive hour.
But e'er you part from blefs'd Britannia's fhore,
And truft your paffage to the golden oar,
To me, O youth, with lift'ning ear attend,
Nor fcorn the leffon of a faithful friend.
When fate fhall land thee on fam'd India's coaft,
Amid an unknown race, thy parents loft—
Thus left in youth thy conduct to direct,
On Life's grand ftage, thy credit to erect,
Beware how thro' the ftormy path of fame,
You fteer aright your yet unblemifh'd name ;
A father's pure example keep in view,
In every action juft, to honor true.
Let virtuous thoughts each vacant hour employ,
And live thy father's pride, thy mother's joy.
And fhould progreffive Time with cautious tread,
E'er place the ruling chaplet on thy head ;
Intwine the laurel wreaths around *thy* brow,
Bid India's fons to *thee* with rev'rence bow,—

And all combin'd, with general one accord,
Should hail thee *Governor !* their *mighty Lord !*
Then crown'd with pow'r— great int'reſt at
        command—
Should *Eaſtern Prince* thy ſervices demand—
Preſent the glaring brilliant to thy ſight,
To tempt thee to his cauſe, or baſe or right;
Reject the bribe, without one moment's thought,
For what corruption gains is dearly bought.
Tell the vain chief, you value virtue more
Than all the gems that grace his glitt'ring ſhore.
Then ev'ry voice your actions will applaud,
" And prove that virtue is its own reward."
Thus will you reign an honor to mankind,
And boaſt the brighteſt gem—a virtuous mind.

    Farewell, then youth! to Heav'n's paternal care,
I yield thee up, with anxious fervent pray'r:—
Ye guardian Pow'rs! this ELEVE fair, receive,
Beneath your guidance, let him prosp'rous live ;
As yet unpoliſh'd in the wiles of Art,
No vice or ſtain pollutes his ſpotleſs heart;
Let not ſuch flow'ret's meet an early doom,
Droop as they ſprout, and wither as they bloom :—

But bid them flourish 'neath the fun's kind ray,
And fcatter bloffoms to eternal day.
Protect them o'er the fea's tempeftuous roar,
And land them fafe on India's fertile fhore;
There let them thrive on her prolific bed,
And when o'er Eaftern realms their fame has fpread,
Perfected by the hand of Induftry,
Unfading grace the Land of Liberty.

STANZAS

ADDRESSED TO A

BRITISH OFFICER,

Separated from his LADY, *by the Fate of War, soon after the*
NUPTIAL DAY.

MY friend! I've often heard thee fay—
   Were I encircl'd midft the fair,
(And *Paris*-like, on Ida's mount)
   To pafs my judgment there.

A wife to choofe— the maid fhould be,
   One with mild attractive pow'r;
To art unknown, of temper kind,
   And form'd in Nature's fmiling hour.

In manners gentle— chafte— and good—
   Fortune has charms— but what care I?
Affection, fenfe, and elegance,
   Shall ev'ry other want fupply.

The vain conceited Mifs, I hate,
   I love the girl from pride that's free;
And Beauty's vifion pleafes more,
   Adorn'd with fweet fimplicity.

The model, thus complete, you view'd,
   What gifts kind Fancy's pow'r beftow'd;
The idol kifs'd— the phantom fpoke,
   And fiction into life has glow'd.

Rejoice, rejoice, the prize admir'd
   Is yours— the nuptial feaft prolong,
Hymen, ftrike the feftive lyre,
   " And fing aloud the bridal fong."

Yet, fate fevere ! by cruel war,
   Thus early torn from her you love !
But *Glory* is the foldier's care,
   And you the foldier's worth fhall prove.

Her heart, too, heaves the frequent figh !
   " When will the fun (fhe hourly cries)
" His tedious hate courfe, have done,
   " And Hefper wake the evening fkies."

But vanquifh'd foon Britannia's foe,
   Behold— ('tis thine) bright Honor's boon !
It fhines around thy conq'ring brow,
   And gilds a *fecond* honey-moon.

Then, bleft return ! Cupid, fportive boy,
    Again Love's path with rofes ftrew;
And as old Time unheard fteals on,
    Let friendfhip thus, their love renew.

'Till, when they view, to glad dull age,
    An offspring dear their fmiles employ,
Reflecting many an happy hour !
    When nought difturb'd Youth's fleeting joy.

Contented reft— let mighty kings
    The fceptre fway of empty blifs;
A far more envied ftate is thine,
    And *yours* the *crown* of happinefs.

VERSES

ON A

BAD DAY.

WHILST round my cot the rude winds blow,
  Content I sit before my fire;
Nor does my soul a trouble know,
  Whilst *they* in mournful plaints conspire.

Hous'd safe within this sweet retreat,
  Ah! what's the tempest's roar to me?
To me, with every joy replete,
  Endow'd with true felicity.

Whilst sullen sportsmen homeward haste,
  My thoughts o'er peerless pleasures rove;
Unmindful of the dreary waste,
  And feast upon the charms of love.

Ah! what's the hound's alluring cry,
  Compar'd to lovely EMMA's voice?
Or, who, in seeing Reynard die,
  Such bliss can boast, or blame my choice?

As now her bofom heaves the figh,
   And confcience pictures Cupid's dart;
I read confeffion in her eye,
   Which fpeaks the language of her heart.

Engag'd in fcenes of fuch delight,
   The gloomy day has charms for me;
Nor could the aid of Sol's gay light,
   Promote fuch pure felicity.

Rail on then, Boreas, what care I !
   Whilft thus I view my love and fire;
What greater blifs beneath the fky,
   Can God permit, or man defire !

THE

FLOWER AND THE INFANT.

WHEN firſt from Nature's pregnant bed
The tender flow'ret rears its head,
   To hail the genial morn;
It bends at every gentle gale,
And ſhrinks within Protection's pale,
   In feeble ſtate forlorn.

But ſtrengthen'd by the hand of Care,
With modeſt, yet majeſtic air,
   It fearleſs views the day;
Secure within the ſafe parterre,
Unconſcious of ſurrounding fear,
   And courts the ſun-beam's ray.

The tempeſt's rage no longer dreads,
Its fragrant ſweets undaunted ſpreads,
   And mocks the Gard'ner's aid;
No preſage threats an early doom,
No wat'ry bed prepares a tomb,
   Of nought, it thrives, afraid.

While many a pleas'd admiring eye,
Behold its odours fcent the fky,
 Exhaling Nature's ftore ;
It grows, fuperior flowers among,
Its praifes blown by many a tongue,
 Are echo'd o'er and o'er.

Thus nurtur'd to Perfection's ftate,
Perhaps too foon eventful fate,
 Befpreads his fnare around ;
Some truant-boy, with mifchief's eyes,
Now wanton views the gaudy prize,
 And plucks it from the ground.

No more in rofeate veft array'd,
In one fhort hour its bloffoms fade,
 Which glitter'd erft fo gay ;
Its beauties flown, its fragrance gone,
He loaths its ruin'd ftate with fcorn,
 And throws the weed away.

Thus, by Creation's happy power's—
But, ah ! more helplefs than the flower's,
 The infant's ftate appears ;
Juft ufher'd into life diftrefs'd,
It mourns, by fecret woes opprefs'd,
 And clad in frequent tears.

In cradle rock'd, or mother's arms,
Awake to fancied Fear's alarms,
   It ſtarts at every ſound;
But ſooth'd its woes, and huſh'd its cries,
With inſtant joy, and glad ſurprize,
   It ſmiles and gazes round.

At length to riper days matur'd,
No more in nurſery immur'd,
   It ſpurns the hand-maid's care;
Like to the Spring's expanding flow'r,
That gathers ſtrength from ev'ry ſhow'r,
   And braves the ſpoiler's ſnare.

Thus blooming forth in virgin ſtate,
With bluſhing pride and heart elate,
   She views the hopeful day;
While native beauty moulds her face,
And many a charm and many a grace,
   Around the idol play.

But, ah! unſkill'd in Vice's art,
Seduction wins her ſimple heart,
   Allures her ſteps aſtray;
Some tempter points where pleaſures reign,
Deceiv'd, ſhe views the roſy plain,
   And quits the thorny way.

His guilty paffion tears approve !
To perjur'd vows of conftant love,
   She falls an eafy prey :
He fteals bright Virtue's pearly gem,
Difgufted views the naufeous ftem,
   And hurls the ftalk away.

THE

SQUIRE's RETURN TO HIS RETREAT.

HAIL! fweet retirement, rural cot!
   Ye violet banks, ye beds of flowers;
Ambrofial fhades— delightful fpot!
   Welcome, welcome, peaceful bowers.

From London's lures releas'd—farewell
   The Mafquerade, the Route, and Ball;
Deign me but this fecreted dell,
   No more I'll tend to Pleafure's call.

No reftlefs nights here rack my mind,
   No taftelefs joys the day devour;
No entrance here does riot find,
   To cloy the fleeting happy hour.

No morning knocks affail the door,
   Announcing Fafhion's num'rous train;
The pamper'd porter waits no more,
   To frown on Poverty difdain.

The fumptuous dinner fmoaks no more,
　　Nor here the Gallic toaft goes round;
No Democrats in frantic roar,
　　Fam'd Revolution's praife refound.

Re-echo'd through Pantheon's rooms,
　　No midnight call rebukes delay;—
Lord *Folly*'s coach, and Lady *Bloom's*,
　　No longer ftop the buftling way.

All here is ftill;—in this retreat,
　　No diffipation dares to rove;
Of blythe content the blifsful feat,
　　And facred to the pureft love.

Here blufhing ANNA tells her tale,
　　And fighs and looks the kindeft things;
While Farmer Blunt applauds the ale,
　　Nor envy we the ftate of Kings.

When Phœbus firft awakes the fkies,
　　And fwallows twitter o'er my head;
Refrefh'd, from true repofe I rife,
　　And quit compos'd my downy bed.

At eve the Shepherd's lute attend,
   Reclin'd the fleecy flocks among;
To PHILOMEL attentive bend,
   And liften to her artlefs fong.

Then foon retiring home to reft,
   (Prepar'd the ftrawberry feaft and cream)
I fink to fleep, completely bleft,
   Immur'd in foft Contentment's dream.

Thus, thus, the rofy minutes fly,
   No care of life my blifs devours;
O, mighty Pow'rs that dwell on high,
   Prolong thefe happy, happy hours.

WRITTEN

ON ELWENA's GRAVE.

NEAR yonder marble tomb, where Folly's name,
Exulting fwells in pompous letter'd fame;
And ftern Ambition's haughty fculptur'd verfe,
The mould'ring inmates mighty deeds rehearfe :—
The loft ELWENA fleeps ! obfcur'd her bed,
No veftige tells where refts her wretched head.
Poor, poor ELWENA ! no memoir of thy date !
Nor weeping friend to mourn thy haplefs fate !
But o'er thy grave, the *fombre*-feated Mufe,
Shall forrowing, penfive ftrains diffufe ;
Efface from memory the direful ftain,
That foil'd thy virtue in its infant reign.—
I heard the bell which fummon'd thy frail duft,
To feek its dark abode in trembling truft ;
I faw thy bier too, carelefs borne along,
Amid the fneerings of th' unfeeling throng :
When fcarce ere Pray'r or Common Service read,
Thy frame was caft unheeding with the dead ;
There to repofe, and wait in awful ftate,
The final fentence of its deftin'd fate.—

Undone ELWENA! accurs'd the mad defire,
That kindled in thy breaft a mutual fire,
That thus entic'd thy willing fteps aftray,
To quit, for Pleafure's path, the thorny way :—
When, lur'd by Flattery, down the fecret bower,
You fell the victim of a guilty hour ;
And, void of honor, virtue, fenfe, and fhame,
Attach'd to lafting infamy your name.—
Yet o'er thy grave I'll drop fome mindful tears,
For ftill this heart thy blafted worth reveres :
Each early morn, o'er thy neglected tomb,
I'll ftrew fweet flow'rets of the choiceft bloom,
Cull'd from the fpot which tempted thy difgrace,
And ftole a ruby, *worlds* could ne'er replace :
For, jealous in that hour, I watch'd thy filent tread,
And view'd thee proftrate on the guilty bed :
Saw the proud tempter clafp thee in his arms,
And feaft in rich delights thy lavifh'd charms:
'Twas there, with Indignation's pow'r I ftrove,
And broke the bond of ill requited love.
Then funk the profpect of a nuptial day ;
I curs'd my folly—tore myfelf away ;
Yet, fleep in peace ! forgivenefs may'ft thou prove,
Awak'd in blifsful Paradife above.

SONNET I.

INVITED oft from Life's dull cares to rove,
 On fome rude precipice I take my ftand ;
There fix'd reflecting on the Powers above,
 I trace the wonders of Creation's hand.

Hufh'd in their caves, the winds in filence fleep,
 Phœbus illumes the mirth-infpiring day ;
As o'er the murm'ring whifpers of the deep,
 He darts in peaceful gleams his filver ray.

Rous'd, as by trumpet's found, the winds arife,
 The angry main affumes a frothy drefs ;
The darken'd profpect wears a black difguife,
 And all around is clad in wild diftrefs !

Thus thoughtful on the wife Almighty's plan,
How vain and lowly feems the ftate of man.

SONNET II.

WHERE haughty Neptune heaves his troubled breaſt,
   And the loud wind mourns o'er the ruffled wave;
On ſome lone beech, I take my ſtand, deprefs'd,
   And ſoothe my ſorrows o'er a wat'ry grave.

Or down the margin of ſome plaintive ſtream,
   By Moon-light's ſolitary dawn I rove;
Watch, playing on the brook, pale CYNTHIA's beam,
   And contemplate in hopelefs thought, my love.

Or, wand'ring o'er the dreary midnight plain,
   To ſome far ivy-colour'd tow'r I ſtray;
Where the dark ſcreech-owl holds his diſmal reign,
   And the black raven wings his boding way.

Yes, yes, thefe gloomy ſcenes to *my* fad heart,
Yield precious balm, and kind relief impart.

SONNET III.

THE night was dark, the tempeſt howl'd around,
  The maniac ſea in loud tremendous roar;
Rag'd wild diſtreſs, with noiſe profound,
  And daſh'd its torrents 'gainſt the rocky ſhore.

The Moon was driven, vanquiſh'd from her reign,
  The dreadful thunder burſted from on high;
The lightning darted o'er the diſtant plain,
  And ſhew'd the horrors of the frightful ſky.

Nor aught was heard! ſave now and then the ſcream
  Of ſhipwreck'd mortals, ſinking to their grave;
Save the dull owl that mop'd its doleful theme,
  And the ſad murmur of the mourning wave.

'Twas then upon the batter'd beach I ſtood,
And watch'd the motions of the raving flood.

SONNET IV.

ON A

DISTANT VIEW OF HARROW SCHOOL.

Written at Windsor.

HAIL! sweet remembrancer of former days,
  Thou kind reflector of my early youth;
Beneath whose learned roof I sought for praise,
  And trod the way to knowledge and to truth.

Alas! ye hills, ye dales, dear haunts of play!
  Ye social walks within yon sacred bow'r,   (L)
Where oft I pictur'd many a happy day,
  And drew false prospects of the future hour!

Where now those friends that swore eternal love,
  Those ties which bound our blended souls in one;
Those vows, then made sincerity to prove,
  E'er vice or pride to sway the heart begun?

Gone are those friends—like visions now they seem,
And nought remains but Life's delusive dream.

SONNET V.

ON THE CLIFF, BEFORE HOLLAND-HOUSE,

IN KENT.

ON fome lov'd margin of the dreadful deep,
  Where fhipwreck'd fragments mark the naked way;
Beneath whofe rude tremendous hanging fteep,
  Bemoaning fea-birds foar in wild difmay:—

And (burfted from their lone-conceal'd recefs)
  The furly winds contending howl along,
O'er the dark waves now foaming mad diftrefs,
  Whofe dafhing threats refound the rocks among:—

And tell triumphant to the lift'ning ear,
  The fate of fome deferted veffel's crew;
Whilft angry furges fad diftinction bear,
  As many a ftorm-left veftige floats to view.

There, there, my deftin'd fteps delight to ftray,
  And court the gloom of black November's day.

SONNET VI.

DEAR infancy,— bleft period of my days!
   When youth's gay fcene was fpread with carelefs
When Peace prefided o'er my blisful lays,   [flow'rs,
   " A child belov'd !— ah, happy, happy hours !"

That ne'er returns, paft feafon of the year !
   And O, falfe hope, that fmil'd to grateful view ;
That oft would dry the troubled fchool-boy's tear,
   And o'er the diftant plain Life's fweets would ftrew.

Scattering, wanton, round, that ne'er would cloy,
   A *thoufand* pleafures waiting Manhood's day;
Where now thofe views of joy, fucceeding joy,
   Delights fubfervient to the paffions' fway !

Thofe profpects bright—thofe joys of life are o'er,
   And vain delufion flatters now no more.

SONNET VII.

SAVILLON

TAKING LEAVE OF ROUBIGNE'S RETREAT.

From the Tale of Julia de Roubigne. (M)

AH, blest retreat! thy shades compell'd to leave,
   Thy grots, thy streams, and paths of rosy hue;
Sweet flow'rs— no more the garland gay to weave,
   Sad mirrors of my happier hours, adieu!

The untrodden glade, to love and virtue dear! (N)
   To friendship sacred, and the fleecy throng;
Where blest SAVILLON pass'd his infant year,
   And JULIA listen'd to the shepherd's song.

Oh! Mem'ry unkind! such scenes thy pow'rs renew,
   Such walks, such thoughts, such blissful days pour-
That youth repines, where happy childhood grew, [tray,
   And looks regardless on Life's future day.

Dreams o'er the past, its many joys to prove,
And tells me *Friendship* was the voice of *Love.*

SONNET VIII.

JULIA

WATERING THE FLOWERS, WHICH SAVILLON HAD PLANTED,
WITH HER TEARS.

From the same. (0)

SECRETED objects of my conftant care !
   I watch'd thee rifing from thy bed of earth ;
Thy odours mark'd perfume the breezy air—
   Ah! plunder'd from the hand that gave them birth.

Thy blufhes glowing on my virgin cheek,
   Love's fatal paffion to my heart reveal'd ;
But, ah ! thy fate fad prefage feems to fpeak,
   Methinks fome cruel danger lurks conceal'd.

Bow'd down beneath rude Autumn's yellow blight,
   Gone are thy blofloms, and thy beauties o'er ;
Dark Winter dooms thee to eternal night,
   May's tranfitory fmile to grace no more.

Yet nurtur'd by a Guardian JULIA's tear,
Thy forms fhall live, reviving with the year.

SONNET IX.

SAVILLON

CONTEMPLATING THE HARDSHIPS OF SLAVERY.

From the same.

THE tortur'd Slave, in bondage born to die,
　Torn weeping, frantic, from his native shore;
Looks forward from the brink of misery,
　As loud he hears the sullen waters roar.

To Night's still moon he silent tells his grief,
　Shakes in despair Oppression's galling chain;
And meditates escape— implores relief—
　But, oh! he meditates— implores in vain!

On no soft breast his suff'rings find repose,
　But, ah, fond hope! he still has life in thee;
Pictures a period to successive woes,
　Nor dreams, alas! of endless slavery.

Yet light to *him* thy many hardships prove,
Who mourns the wound of secret, untold love.

SONNET X.

SAVILLON

ON THE DEATH OF HIS FRIEND BEAUVARIS.

From the fame.

OH, Hope deceitful! while o'er diftant feas,
   Thy faded bloffoms to the fenfes bloom;
Death, heedlefs fleets along the moaning breeze,
   And haggard Poverty prepares a tomb. (P)

Lamented worth of Friendfhip's early hour!
   An heart was thine— to pity facred, and to truth
The foother kind of Love's corroding power, [fincere:
   And pure afylum of Affliction's tear.

As quits the preffure of Life's ftormy night,
   The man, whofe fecret lofs no friends deplore;
So finks thy excellence from earthly fight,
   Remember'd by an haughty world no more.

But the bright emblem fhall SAVILLON fave,
And fnatch thy virtues from Oblivion's grave.

SONNET XI.

JULIA

WEEPING OVER THE PICTURE OF SAVILLON.

From the same.

DEAR, cherifh'd image of my childifh love!
 Or, Friendfhip's vifion, fhall I call it thine?
Ah, fond refemblance! can reflection prove,
 That *childifh* love, and friendfhip, ftill are mine?

In JULIA's bofom is it guilt to lie?
 On thy pale cheek to drop a thoughtful tear—
From the wet glafs to wipe the mifty figh—
 O Prudence, dictate to my doubtful ear.

Another's wife! SAVILLON, in one look,
 The facred tie of wedlock do I break?
Like the fick fwain, that views the moony brook,
 'Tis but a momentary glance I take.

Yes, Honor frowns—but come, propitious fhine,
Hence, Virtue, and MONTAUBAN, I am thine.

SONNET XII.

SAVILLON

PROCURES A LAST INTERVIEW WITH JULIA, AND DETERMINES ON
LEAVING HIS NATIVE COUNTRY FOR EVER.

From the fame.

FAR from the fmile of Titan's cheering ray,
  'Crofs the Atlantic fhall SAVILLON rove;
There feek fome folitude—to grief a prey—
  " The wretched martyr of unhappy love."

Ah, JULIA! JULIA! each vifionary joy,
  Of Love's lorn hope, Life's darker clouds difpel;
Riches no more my anxious thoughts employ,
  Dear plans of worldly happinefs, farewell!

On calm Religion's prop reclin'd at laft,
  I'll drown affliction with futurity;
Like the poor maniac fool, forget the paft,
  Weave my ftraw crown, and laugh at mifery.

Thus the wreck'd veffel, by the tempeft toft,
Mocks the mad wave, when ev'ry hope is loft.

SONNET XIII.

MONTAUBAN

MEDITATING THE DEATH OF HIS WIFE JULIA.

From the same. (Q)

AWAY, away, the joys of foolifh love!
  This injur'd breaft no more the figh fhall heave;
Honor directs— and Juftice from above,
  O, tell me, fhould the guilty JULIA live?

Curs'd jealoufy! doubts like vifions feem—
  While in a hufband's arms carefs'd fhe lies;
SAVILLON revels in the wanton dream,
  The picture too?— refolv'd, refolv'd,— fhe dies.

Her trembling hand the fatal cup receives—
  Down, down my fenfes to their deftin'd hell;
Now to her lip— MONTAUBAN's health fhe breathes;
  She drinks! fhe drinks! the deed is done, farewell!

Rewarded now, my high revengeful foul,
Gluts its proud paffion o'er the poifon'd bowl.

SONNET XIV.

JULIA,

IN HER LAST LETTER TO MARIA. (2)

From the same.

FAREWEL, MARIA! on Life's dull chequer'd shore,
　For *thee* may many a spring its sweets renew;
To *me* her vernal joys return no more,—
　Lost, lost SAVILLON, and the world, adieu!

"Oh! name for ever sad, for ever dear!"
　In JULIA's latest breath thy accents live;
But soon the heavy sigh, the struggling tear,
　Their pangs to memory shall cease to give.

Wild madness seizes on my troubled brain!—
　Big horrors warn me of approaching fate;
Poor sick SAVILLON joins the funeral train,
　"As now I enter Death's dark gate,"

Prostrate he lays upon my midnight cell,
He raves, he storms, distraction! death! farewell!!!

SAVILLON

AT THE

TOMB OF JULIA. (s)

COME ye, whofe gloomy thoughts thro' darknefs
   Whofe fated fteps purfue the track of woe; [rove,
Ye hearts, yet burning with the flame of love,
   Here heal with grief the wound of Mis'ry's blow.

Come, ftalk with me, along this vaulted roof,
   Where flumb'ring reft beneath the filent dead;
Here fix your tenement, a facred proof,
   That Sorrow reigns the partner of your bed.

Ye youth! whoe'er a JULIA's love could boaft—
   Stript in the budding blow of early bloom!
Here hold your converfe with the nightly ghoft,
   Which Fancy iffues from this honor'd tomb.

Hence from the couch that courts the lover's lay,
   On this cold ftone I'll fix my drear abode;
Where no fond Cupids fport in wanton play,
   Or pleafures eafe me from Affliction's load.

On this cold stone I'll fix my drear abode!

Here will I quaff the cup of baleful grief,
   And fwill, in copious drafts, luxurious woe;
Here from the fleeping dead I'll claim relief,
   And as the dew-drop falls, *my* tears fhall flow.

Each morn this fpot with rofes will I ftrew,—
   This fculptur'd buft fhall be my lonely gueft;
By moonlight here I'll fit, beneath this Yew,
   And woo the fting of forrow to my breaft.

Yea, here my fteps fhall ceafe their wearied roam,
   And ftalk in fable Melancholy's train;
Oft fhall they prefs with grief this hallow'd tomb,
   And found thefe echoing vaults in plaintive ftrain.

Here by this urn my head fhall feek repofe,
   And lull to balmy reft thefe grief-fwoln eyes;
Here fhall my forrow fleep, forgot my woes,
   'Till Death fhall lay me, where my JULIA lies.

MARIA,

AN ELEGY,

FOUNDED ON AN INSCRIPTION, IN A COUNTRY CHURCH-YARD.

THIS wafted frame, this breaft that heaves the figh,
　Adown this vifage pale, the tears that flow ;
This head which long in reft has ceas'd to lie,
　Profefs a heart, no ftranger fure to woe.

Ah ! long this breaft has forrow doom'd to pain,
　And oft to pant beneath Affliction's load ;
In vain thefe limbs have ftrove new ftrength to gain,
　To find relief within their loft abode.

And long too, Melancholy, fable gueft,
　Here woo'd, has fix'd her grief devoted reign ;
And lur'd my footfteps from the path of reft,
　To join her penfive folitary train.

And long thefe eyes, thro' darknefs doom'd to rove,
　Have banifh'd from their fight the Sun's glad beam;
And floating down the moon-light tide of love,
　Have read each forrow in the limpid ftream.

Oft too, by night, they've fought the church-yard
  To foothe their forrows at MARIA's fhrine; [drear,
And, dropping o'er her bed the balmy tear,
  Have bath'd the fod where Beauty fleeps divine.

Then mufing penfive on the fculptur'd buft,
  Which breathes in letter'd traits her matchlefs fame;
How have they lav'd with Pity's dew the duft,
  That kindred, mingles with her mould'ring frame!

Ah! ne'er a fairer face! a purer mind!
  Did Virtue form, or Nature's hand engrave ;
Ah! ne'er fuch fenfe, with *beauty* was combin'd—
  Heav'n ne'er before fuch worth to mortal gave.

But to Love's tale, an harmlefs ear fhe lent,
  To perjur'd man, fhe liften'd and believ'd ;
Nor fcarce had tafted vice, when fore repent,
  Her bofom pierc'd, too late, alas! deceiv'd.

Heav'n thus witnefling her child's difgrace,
  Her peace thus flain by man's regardlefs hand;
It foon recall'd her to her native place,
  By Angels beckon'd from Corruption's land.

And there, MARIA ! may'ſt thou find repoſe,
   And happy, bleſt eternity enjoy :
There may thy burthen'd ſoul (reliev'd its woes)
   True pleaſure prove, and nought its reſt annoy.

Oh, there, may this fond heart from torture ceaſe,
   And join'd with thine, forget its every grief ;
For you *alone*, its ſorrows can appeaſe—
   For you *alone*, can yield this heart relief !

THE

BRITISH PRISONER,

AT SERINGAPATAM.

Written during the late War with Tippoo Sultan, *when* Lord
Cornwallis *was supposed to be on his march to the Capital of this*
Eastern Prince.

WITHIN thefe fenfelefs walls of ftone,
A wretched Captive doom'd to moan,
　　Beneath a Monfter's fway ;—
Oh, tell me, Hope, if e'er again,
Thy profp'rous rays will foothe my pain,
　　And lead to life the way ?

Ye flow'ry fields of Albion's fhore,
O, fhall I ne'er behold thee more,
　　Nor hail my native land ?
Ah ! like the flave of Afric's coaft,
To deareft friends and country loft,
　　I view the diftant ftrand.

Every hour frefh terror brings,
Death with all its goading ftings,
　　Opprefs the mind with fear ;
Perhaps, e'en now in torment ftate,
Some haplefs Chriftian meets his fate,
　　Extorting many a tear.

O Prefage kind, *my* fate unroll—
Is it by rope, or poifon'd bowl,
   A wretch is doom'd to die?
Or does the Tyrant's will ordain,
His victim, mangled, to fuftain
   A life of mifery?

Sad emblems of my future fate,
What forms of death my fancy wait,
   Within this lonely cell!
Now iffued forth the dire decree—
Methinks I hear the Tyrant's plea,
   Revenge! Revenge!— farewell!

Yet, hark!— the trumpet's fhout I hear—
Victory! Victory! greets the ear—
   'Twas Britain's voice I heard;—
See, fee, the Tyrant Monfter's dead,
The brave *Cornwallis* bears his head,
   Amid the vanquifh'd herd.

Meadows, behold, unknown to dread,
His laurels waving o'er the dead,
   With reeking fpear in hand;
Whilft many a Chief, by vengeance flain,
Expiring fwells the crimfon plain,
   A debt to Albion's land.

The deeds this day by Britons won,
Shall gild each morning's rifing fun,
   More fplendid for his rays ;
Humanity with-holds her tear,
No tortur'd deaths affright the ear,
   Or kindred forrow raife.

Bleft hour ! that decks with Conqueft's name,
Th' hiftoric page of England's fame,
   And life reftores to me ;—
Such honors gain'd by warfare's broil,
Embalms the fons of Albion's foil,
   Examples to pofterity.

TRIBUTARY LINES,

ON THE ARRIVAL OF

MARQUIS CORNWALLIS,

FROM INDIA.

THRICE welcome Champion to your native ifle :
The trumpet fhouts applaufe,— the people fmile—
Accept, O Chief belov'd, the Nation's kifs,
Return with mutual joy their happinefs.—
Tho' India's fons in tribes their lofs deplore,
The *Ifland's* happy children weep no more.

On Albion's cliff was heard the mournful tale,
(There wafted by fome fympathizing gale)
How groups fat thoughtful on the Eaftern fhore,
And anxious watch'd the gloom-infpiring oar,
That forc'd from Friendfhip's arms the man rever'd,
As thro' repelling waves, a courfe it fteer'd :
When (fafe on board) the parting fwallow heav'd a
      figh, (T)
Long may he live ! God blefs him ! was the blended cry.
While flow'd adown each cheek the gen'rous tear,
That filent teftified the heart fincere ;

Sorrows burſt, frantic, from the moaning deep,
And Pity rous'd the ſurge— beat rocks to weep;
While from their lofty tops in diſmal reign,
The wretched ſea-bird pour'd his plaintive ſtrain,
'Till the far ſail, upon the ocean toſt,
A farewell bow'd— and ev'ry hope was loſt.

On Hiſt'ry's ſacred leaf ſhall live *that* day,
When Britain's flag, in mild triumphant play,
'Mid TIPPOO's vanquiſh'd troop its vict'ry told,
Demanding *Juſtice* from the Tyrant bold;
When England's Chief compell'd the treaty ſign'd,
And taught ſubmiſſion to his haughty mind;
That day which India's broken reſt reſtor'd,
And ſheath'd, in peace approv'd, the Lion's ſword:—
Proud fragments ſcatt'ring from the Sultan's plain,
The ruin'd emblems of Britannia's gain;
On which her ſons ſhall riſe to brighter fame,
And bleſs with thanks, their Indian-Saviour's name.

No cringing flatterer is *He*, who now
In humble verſe around thy martial brow,
(No eaſy taſk) the bluſhing garland twines;
Where Britain's glorious ſun immortal ſhines;
Let *others* deck with *gems* the warrior's crown,
Enough for *me*, the ſimple wreath to own,

Which fhows more grateful to his noble view,
When Nature proves the modeft off'ring true.
But, when in Death's foft fleep the bafhful ear,
No more the din of Eulogy can fear;
When, full of years, remov'd by Heav'n's decree
To happier regions of eternity!
Then will a *Pope* arife, and o'er the tomb
Thy warlike deeds, and private worth fhall bloom,
On record fhine— admir'd by diftant age,
And gild with fplendid truth the Poet's page.

VERSES

ON THE DREADFUL FIRE, AT RATCLIFFE.

ATTEND, oh Grief! be thou my penfive guide,
Thro' the dark fcene and defolation wide;
Where RATCLIFFE's afhes fcent the murky air,
And loud is heard the figh of deep defpair.
What havoc marks the rude obftructed way,
Where Mifchief unappall'd extends her fway!
Yon reeking pile behold! the ruin'd fpot,
Where lately flood the Peafant's humble cot;
There Induftry had plac'd its downy bed,
And rais'd a pillow for the weary head.
(Still flatter'd with the hopes of precious life)
The worn-out hufband, and the fickly wife,
Endeav'ring to fecure their flender all,
Lie crufh'd beneath the roof's tremendous fall!
Whilft unalarm'd the milky fource it prefs'd,
The tortur'd babe finks fcreaming from the breaft;
Torn from the tafk of foft parental care,
The mother fhrieks, and frantic, rends her hair;
Her boafted, only pride— the father's joy—
'Mid the fierce flames behold their darling boy;

Ah ! what avail the wretched parents' cries—
Disfigur'd, loft, a parch'd up corpfe he lies !—
There raves the fon diftracted thro' the fire,
Imploring mercy for his aged Sire ;
Here ragged orphans, thro' the fragments creep,
Their kindred trace, and o'er their parents weep.—
The virgin gone; to death an early prey—
To morrow's fun had blefs'd the bridal day ;
See, fee the fwain, to virtuous paffion true,
Her frame unfolds, and bids a laft adieu.
In vain for *him* the voice of comfort cries,
For *him* no more a happy morn fhall rife.
Hark ! burfting from the mournful widow'd train,
What groans are heard along the troubled plain !
The bell tolls forth ! ah! number'd with the dead,
Is *fhe* who us'd to prop the forrowing head:—
Who now will guard the unprotected poor,
" And yield a pittance from their ample ftore ?"
Ye tribes reliev'd,— to you thefe rites belong—
Strike the fad lyre, and found the fun'ral fong ;
While o'er her grave, to grace the folemn hour,
The *Stranger* weeps— a teft of Virtue's power !
Ah ! many more in rueful, black array,
Will long lament the inaufpicious day,

That o'er fweet Concord fpread its awful gloom,
And fentenc'd Friendfhip to a filent tomb.
Shall painful Mem'ry then, unheard deplore
The fate of deareft relatives no more?
Can Britain's genuine fons unmov'd, behold
Thefe difmal fcenes the Mufe has feebly told,
And yet deny a tributary tear,
To deck the good man's hearfe— the infant's bier ?
Still further does their gen'rous bounty flow,
To ftem the torrent of furrounding woe;
As when fufpended from the drooping rofe,
With weight o'erwhelm'd the modeft dew-drop flows,
Reviv'd beneath Sol's tranfitory ray,
More bright it glitters to the dreary day.
So falls untutor'd, from the furcharg'd eye,
The balmy tear of Britifh fympathy:
And claims relation to the chryftal flower,
When facred *Charity* beftows the dower.

LINES

TO A

YOUNG LADY,

(UNDER MISFORTUNES) ON HER BIRTH-DAY, WITH THE PRESENT

OF A POCKET BOOK.

ELIZA, dear! this mindful day
Gave birth to thee— I think they fay—
Take then this trifle ;— let it prove
A token of eternal love.
That love, which conftant, pure, and true,
My facred bofom early knew.
When Fortune frown'd around thy bed,
And Life's endearing fweets were fled,
Then firft I felt Affection's pow'r,
And view'd thee like a blighted flow'r,
Juft funk beneath the cruel ftorm,
And plunder'd of its graceful form !
No more in brilliant fair array,
To emulate the gifts of May.
But Phœbus ftill fhall prop the ftem,
Tho' robb'd of Admiration's gem.

Oh, may he ne'er deny his rays,
But gild with peace thy future days:
May genuine blifs each hour beguile,
And virtue live in Wifdom's fmile:
Still Life's misfortunes be forgot,
And bleft contentment e'er thy lot.

ADDRESSED to the AUTHOR,

FROM G. W. ESQ.

WHEN firſt the ſnow-drop rears its infant head,
By rural mildneſs nurtur'd in the mead,
Leſt ſome rude breeze its tender bloom confound,
It bends in modeſt meekneſs to the ground:
Improv'd in vigor, and matur'd by age,
Fearleſs it views the tempeſt's tranſient rage,
Courts unabaſh'd the ſun's all genial ray,
And ſpreads its brighteſt beauties to the day.
So the firſt efforts of thy modeſt worth,
In humble chaſteneſs puſh its bloſſoms forth:
Untry'd thoſe pow'rs which Nature form'd to pleaſe,
They droop and tremble at the ſlighteſt breeze.—
By judgment ripen'd— the firſt trial paſt,
Boldly they'll brave the rudeſt Critic blaſt,
Burſt forth in beauty like ethereal light,
And ſtrike with peerleſs tints th' aſtoniſh'd ſight.

FROM THE SAME TO THE SAME.

O, STREPHON! attune thy foft reed,
  To accents more cheerful and gay;
Too much haft thou made the heart bleed,
  Too oft has it wept at thy lay.—

Ah! ceafe for LOUISA the tear,
  Ah! ceafe for MARIA to mourn;
Nor wafte in the fpring of thy year,
  Thofe hours which can never return.

Go join the brifk dance on the green,
  Attend the gay nightingale's fong;—
See, Health prefides over the fcene,
  See, Pleafure enlivens the throng.—

Go, tafte the rich juice of the vine,
  Of innocent mirth be the gueft;
Thy wit fhall give zeft to the wine,
  Thy good humour fhall feafon the jeft.

LETTER

TO A

KENTISH FARMER,

WITH

AN EPITAPH.

SIR,

BEING in your neighbourhood a few days ago, when taking an evening's walk, I happened to ſtroll into Footſcray Church-yard.— Led into a train of thinking, occaſioned by the ſo-lemnity of the ſcene, and, contemplating the tran-ſitory, uncertain ſtate of this world, together with the many ups and downs attendant on man in his paſſage through life; among other circum-ſtances which ſtruck my imagination, a yew-tree, very neatly fenced round with white railing, was one, not the leaſt attended to; and being informed, (upon enquiry) by a perſon who was juſt then paſſ-ing near the place, that it was the ſpot, where, (when it pleaſed God to deprive your friends of the pleaſure which your ſociety affords them) you deſign your remains ſhall be depoſited: I was a good deal

interefted at the intelligence, and queftioned the
ftranger further as to the character of JOHN T——,
and finding it agreeable to my expectations, I reclined upon an oppofite buft, (having the back of a
letter, with a pencil in my pocket) and wrote the in-
clofed Epitaph, fuppofing at the inftant, the event to
have occurred; though, I hope the time (when the
fubject which gave rife to the lines in queftion fhall
be verified) is yet at a diftant period.

The tranfcript therefore, which I have been
induced to fend you, proceeds merely from a defire
to teftify the eftimation in which you are held by
fome people, and not from an idea that any merit
(fave that of regard) is attached to the performance.

I remain, Sir,

LONDON, *May* 10, 1791.

Yours, &c. &c.

EPITAPH. (v)

LAMENTED, here, beneath this yew-tree's fhade,
The height of human excellence is laid :
Tho' wealth, tho' honors, fmil'd not on his birth,
Him few could equal— *none* furpafs in worth;
Blamelefs, he travers'd Life's intricate ways,
And left his actions to his Maker's praife !
Weep, then ye, who worth, who virtue prize,
For worth with virtue here congenial lies.
Yet flumb'ring only refts his guiltlefs head,
Awak'd, again, he'll quit this earthly bed;
When the high Lord his mighty trump fhall found,
He'll foar to Heav'n, where the juft are crown'd !
Ye then who read, and hope for Virtue's fame,
Purfue his fteps— revere his righteous name.

(Signed)   A PASSER-BY.

EPITAPH,

ON THE AUTHOR'S SISTER.

DID Friendſhip's tear— fair Virtue's pow'r—
　Did Beauty's grace, or fond parental care,
Avail in Death's afflicting hour:—
　No teſt would here the mournful truth declare,
How vain, how ſhort's the youthful virgin's bloom!
How often deſtin'd to an early tomb!

LINES

TO THE MEMORY OF

THOMAS R—MB——D, ESQ.

Who died of a FEVER, *in the Twenty-third Year of his Age, lamented
and beloved. Written by an impartial Admirer of his departed Worth.*

OH, Memory ! juft mirror of the paft,
When joys are flown, and only forrows laft ;—
If e'er a tribute at thy fhrine was due,
To modeft Worth— to Pity— or to Genius true ;
O'er loft, lamented R—MB——D's filent urn,
Thy facred gifts fhall unextinguifh'd burn :
Kind youth ! to thee belongs the pearly boon,
(Snatch'd from a weeping world, alas ! too foon)
And, ah ! how bright the gem which *ftrangers* fhed,
O'er the poor relics of the virtuous dead !
No tongue I need thy qualities to prove—
I read thy lift of virtues in a parent's love,—
A Mother's Hufband and a Sifter's Sire !
Thefe light the Mufes' fympathetic fire ;

No art was thine, except the art to pleaſe;
No leſs'ning vice— ſo candid Juſtice ſays:
O ye, who knew that Son the Almighty gave,
There, view him, bearing to an early grave !
Go mingle dirges with the diſmal train,
And chant his worth— " ah! never to return
        again!"
See, a fond Siſter's fair religious tear,
Wets the lov'd duſt, and bathes the funeral bier !
Ah, thence glad parents learn, ere yet too late,
Of mortal happineſs how vain's the ſtate;
How ſoon are humbled thoſe, who, of their ſons are
        proud,
How ſoon is each perfeĉtion buried in the ſhroud !
How deareſt wiſhes fail— are chang'd to grief—
Then ſeek the widow's couch with calm relief;
And ſay— howe'er the proſp'rous bleſſings can,
No *earthly* bliſs e'er recompens'd the cares of man;
O ſay, the child, her ſobs, her ſighs bemoan,
Quits a ſtain'd land to grace his Maker's throne ;
But, ah ! too recent yet, the tender ſore,
Dreads the ſoft touch, when comfort is no more;
Let Time, beſt balm for ev'ry human woe,
Aſſuage thoſe pangs, the ſuff'rers only know;

While Refignation's pow'rs their aid fhall give,
With hopes, that after death, the righteous live:
Lo ! his pure fpirit, lifted up on high,
Smiles thro' the realms of Immortality!
Wipes from each kindred cheek Affliction's drop,
And fubftitutes the faithful Chriftian's prop.

And there the Infant sleeps within the tomb,
  Ere scarce he'd sip'd the care-mix'd drop of life
Here too the Husband meets an early doom!
  And here forgotten rests the virtuous Wife.

VERSES

ON

A CHURCH-YARD, AT MOON-LIGHT.

BE calm, my thoughts, whilſt thro' this manſion
   In penſive meditation loſt I ſtray;   [dread,
Whilſt thro' theſe dreary regions of the dead,
   With pauſing ſtep I take my lonely way.

How fair the Moon! majeſtic Queen of Night!
   Enthron'd on high, amid her ſtarry train;
How awful gleams her ſilver orb of light,
   Thro' theſe ſad haunts of ſolitary reign!

What ſtillneſs dwells the ſolemn ſcene around!
   O'er theſe dark tenements of ſilent reſt;
What fears and doubts my wand'ring ſoul confound!
   Alas! what terrors croud within my breaſt!

Ah! grave! thou dread, yet ſure abode of all;
   Thou final bar to heedleſs man's career;
The monarch and the ſlave muſt tend *thy* call,
   Alike each trembles at thy name with fear.

No *royal* pillow here awaits the head,
　　Nor here repose the limbs the stately chair;
All herd together in one common bed,
　　Alike the *Beggar's* and the *Prince's* fare.

What now avail Ambition's fleeting charms,
　　The star-deck'd vest— the showy titled car;
The grave, each inmate of his pride disarms,
　　When conq'ring Death extends his massy bar.

Where now the pride which gilds this sculptur'd bust,
　　That tells in pompous traits the warrior's fame?
His bones and deeds lay mould'ring with the dust,
　　Here fall his honors, and here dies his name. (v)

Where now the arm that hurl'd the well-aim'd dart,
　　And gleam'd its threat'ning terrors o'er the land?
The fatal spear which pierc'd the dauntless heart,
　　Now lies unbrandish'd by his nervelefs hand.

And here the *Statesman* rests, for sense renown'd,
　　No more the patriot listens to his laws;
Here lies his worth entomb'd within the ground,
　　Nor echoes now his voice in Freedom's cause.

And there the *Infant* sleeps within the tomb,
  Ere scarce he'd sip'd the care-mix'd drop of life ;
Here too, the husband meets an early doom !
  And here, forgotten, rests the virtuous wife !

Mingled together, disregarded lie,
  The husband, wife, child, monarch, and the slave;
At Death's command all pride, all honors die,
  Nor lives distinction in the humble grave.

Alas ! ye tenants of these darksome cells,
  Can'st tell, if lasting sleep your eyelids close ?—
If in thy caverns *happiness* e'er dwells,
  Do ye not dream, or wakeless here repose ?

For why, if here, Life's many troubles end,
  Should man thus dread Death's summons to obey ?
Why not impute his messenger a friend,
  That pitying warns him to his native clay ?

But there's the doubt that stops my soul's career,
  And bids it from a fruitless travel cease;
In vain it strives the mazy course to steer,
  For wand'ring as it soars, the mists increase.

Quit then, my toilſome ſteps, this hallow'd ground,
 Nor from your mark'd-out bounds unheeding ſtray;
No longer ſtalk in vain theſe tombs around,
 But homeward from the dead, re-ſeek your way.

Nor hence, my lawleſs ſoul, your flight betake,
 On duſky pinions thro' the darken'd ſky;
Bend not your courſe (intelligence to make)
 Thro' night, alas! unknowing where to fly!

Dwell, then, ſweet peace, within this ſacred *fane*;
 Thus undiſturb'd ye manes, forgotten reſt;
Let not this hidden ſecret rack my brain,
 'Till Death reveals it to my anxious breaſt.

THE

COTTAGE in the VALE.

BLEST Cottage, hail!
In peaceful vale,
Of ev'ry joy possefs'd;
Where nature sports,
Retir'd from courts,
And gives to life a zest.

Soft glides each hour
Thro' thy sweet bow'r,
Nor chides the Sun's delay;
But shines too soon
The silv'ry Moon,
To mourn departed day.

Hail! calm retreat!
True Wisdom's seat!
Unknown to Folly's train:
From vices free,
Content there see,
Has fix'd her favor'd reign.

J—NS—N to you,
The bard is true,
Who sings thy worth to raise;
Who tunes his lyre,
O, happy Sire,
To sound thy Consort's praise.

For what can be,
More blythe to see,
Fond parents *sans* despair;
As sweet they sip,
From children's lip,
The kiss uncloy'd by care.

Envious state!
The haughty Great
Must yield the prize to thee;
Nor search in vain
The Peer's domain,
For perfect harmony.

No gay parade,
Or masquerade,
Nor op'ra, ball, nor play;
Can boast delight,
So pure and bright,
To banish spleen away.

O, filent vale !
O, happy dale !
Where J——NS——N fits entwin'd,
Amid the woods,
A feat for Gods,
Enjoying peace of mind.

Ye rofeate bow'rs !
Ye fragrant flow'rs !
That in the valley dwell ;
My theme fhall be,
To fing of thee,
And how thy fweets excel.

The buftling ftrife,
Of fafhion'd life,
And all the gay call blifs ;
To thee refign,
To thee confign
The crown of happinefs.

" O, life of blifs !
" To equal this,
" Proud Fafhion ftrives in vain ;
" O, happy pair !
" O, happy fair !
" O, happy, happy fwain."

SOLAR ECLIPSE.

STANZAS

Occasioned by the WEST KENT COLOURS, *a Present from Her Grace the* DUTCHESS *of* DORSET, *being first produced in Camp, at Harwich, on the above Day; September* 5, 1793.

THAT day shall mem'ry oft call o'er,
When prais'd aloud the Kentish corps,
   Their Chieftain's grateful name:
And blest by ev'ry soldier's tongue,
In air his Consort's worth they sung,
   Whose deeds like homage claim.

Thus, glitt'ring o'er the warlike plain,
Fair Virtue's Ensign view'd the train,   (w)
   Bearing her gift along,
By peerless female taste prepar'd:—
The neighing steed the boon declar'd,
   And hail'd the loyal throng.

The standard rais'd,— as tho' by chance,
The Sun bestowing one proud glance,
   Abash'd his radiance hid:
In modest grace the colours play'd,
A conscious blush their pow'rs pourtray'd,
   Which Sol's feint rays forbid.

While joyous 'mid the trumpet's found,
In hafty march affembling round ;
   Brave KENT's intrepid band :—
The darken'd fky their vifion caught !
They gaz'd— proclaim'd the wonder wrought
   By lovely DORSET's hand.

CHOICE of a WIFE.

THIS morn, when muſing on the ſcenes of life,
I fondly drew the model of a wife:
Her form was elegant, her dreſs was neat,
Her manners gentle, and her temper ſweet:
Wrought by Nature with peculiar care,
As pure DIANA chaſte— as HELEN fair:—
In ſhort, all things were form'd to man's deſire,
To fan the blaze— to animate the fire,—
But what, thought I, as beauty fades away,
Will there remain to ſmoothe Life's wintry day?
I then perus'd the beauties of her *mind*,
And genius found, with ſentiments refin'd:
Not proud— learned enough— yet not *too* wiſe;
Her inward worth wore Modeſty's diſguiſe;
Religion, Truth, and Charity conſpir'd,
To grace her mind, in every ſenſe attir'd.
Such was the fair one which my fancy drew,
But, when I held her likeneſs up to view,
And on the picture gaz'd— vain wiſh, I cry'd,
An *Angel* ne'er on earth did yet reſide.
Truth, then whiſp'ring ſaid, but this *can* be,
For all theſe requiſites in ——— you'll ſee.

ADIEU to COLLEGE.

FAREWELL, *drear* College, and thy binding rules;
At once the seat of scholars— and of fools ;
Where fancy paints each student in his room,
With books encircl'd, 'mid the Cloister's gloom ;
In *Locke* wrapt up— or lost in *Newton's* lore,
The heav'nly regions striving to explore ;
But oft'ner where, in Bacchanalian roar,
His comrades meet, to prove the cellar's store.

 Adieu, ye motley scenes, ye tasteless joys,
Thy dull insipid sameness daily cloys :—
No more the Chapel-bell shall break my rest,
Or threat'ning raise commotion in my breast ;
Nor from the social board, to ev'ning pray'r,
Shall its lone accents bid my steps repair:
The surly porter at the midnight gate,
No more shall bid me College vengeance wait;
No more enrol me in the nightly list,
Unless the *Fee* should tempt him to desist.
Nor hence shall morning duns my door assail,
To paint distress in Sorrow's woeful tale.

Lord *Dash*, Sir William *Squander*, and fome more,
Have fled! and left a moft enormous fcore;
Pity my cafe, and let my wants prevail:—
With your kind heart, I'm fure they cannot fail—
Begone, ye canting tribe, with vifage pale!
You've drain'd my pocket with your mournful tale. .
My tinfel'd gown, farewell! no more to grace
My difrob'd perfon with thy tawdry lace:
Stript of my plumage and my honors fled,
No more the golden taffel decks my head,
No longer courts obeifance from the throng,
Or *bows* from Fellows as I pafs along.
Nor longer now, the tutor, fage divine,
My bills will ftretch, or praife my London wine; (x)
On fome new velvet cap, with *fmirking face*,
His views he'll fix, and bow with *abject grace*.—
The prying proctor, too, the *mean-earn'd* fee (y)
No more fhall force, to prove his poverty:
Nor hence fhall bid me tend his ftern commands,
Or wait forgivenefs, at his *gen'rous* hands.

And thou, fam'd FRANK! with cheeks of crimfon
          hue, (z)
Thou true-born fon of Impudence, adieu!
No more thy wit and ready joke to fhare,
Or bid fweet SALLY tea and toaft prepare.

My comrades too, farewell! no more to join,
In College pranks, or fwill thy muddy wine:
No more to hear the noify fongfter's roar,
Or witnefs drunkards fleeping on the floor.

Such taftelefs joys no real blifs afford,
Where vice, inftead of pleafure crowns the board:
Where no decorum fways the fenfelefs throng,
Nor lovely woman checks the boundlefs tongue:
But Bacchus, unmolefted, holds his reign,
And dulls, with *too much* wine, the fumy brain.

Be mine the fate far happier fcenes to prove,
To boaft the prize of fome fair maiden's love!
May time quick kindle in my breaft the flame,
Quick fpread its gen'rous ardour thro' my frame:
Then Cupid aim thy well-directed dart,
And fix it deep in her congenial heart:
Thence may we fip the balm of pureft love,
Decreed eternal happinefs to prove.

F I N I S.

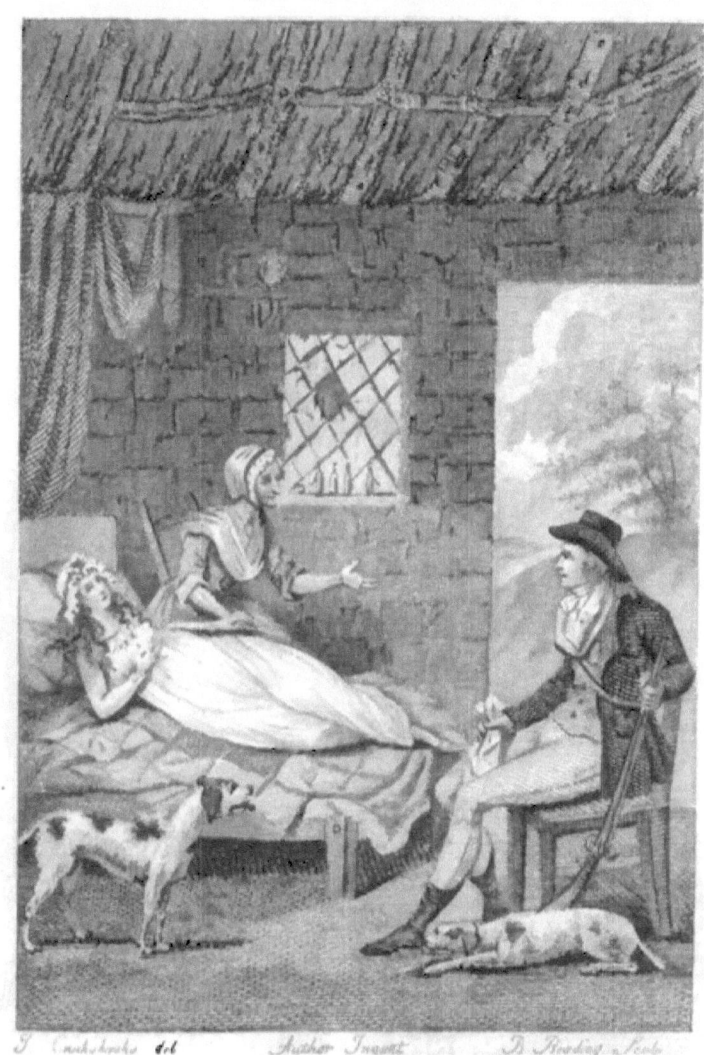

I. Cruikshanks del.   Author Invent.   B. Reading Sculp.

Alas, Maria!

But scarce had she culled the glaring flowers of Vice,
Than withering in her hand, she hurled them from her &
returned disgusted from the gaudy path,
And sought again repenting the tracks of Virtue.

THE
SYMPATHIZING SPORTSMAN;
OR,
THE COTTAGE OF MISFORTUNE.

A SENTIMENTAL FRAGMENT.

IT was a burning firſt of September—I had taken a ſporting box for a couple of months at a conſiderable diſtance from the metropolis, in the county of ————, and had riſen at dawn of day, to enjoy a diverſion, to which from my early youth I had been immoderately attached. Being maſter of two brace of pointers, it was my plan to hunt them alternately. Don and Plato were my companions fixed upon to welcome Aurora's beams, and to uſher in the ſeaſon; it is not here neceſſary to detail their qualities, ſuffice it to obſerve, they were ſuch dogs in the aggregate as few ſportſmen could boaſt.

The game was scarce, and the harvest backward, and I had fagged along till noon, without being gratified by a single point:— despairing of success, and a good deal fatigued, I reclined upon a stile, in that languid state of suspense, which a sportsman feels when disappointed in his expectations, and contemplating his future plan. The scene around was calculated to inspire reflection, being romantic and picturesque; on each side were fields of waving corn, behind a woody dell, at the bottom of which a bubbling stream softly murmured its irregular course: the prospect before presented a grassy lawn, about a mile in extent, intersersed with spreading oaks, and here and there, stood a solitary shrub, a sad remnant, as it seemed, to tell the enquiring passenger that the spot had formerly been the residence of grandeur and magnificence.

Pleased with the delightful solitude, it was some time before I discovered a small cottage, which raised its humble top, situated upon a rising slope, at the extreme verge of that lawn I have described.— Undetermined as to my future route, added to a total ignorance of the country, I was induced on the score of information to approach it; besides, a material part of my apparatus, through eagerness in

the morning to commence the fport, had been forgotten; it was my leather bottle filled with choice
Madeira, that had thrice voyaged it round the Cape,
and which I had placed on the table a few minutes
only before my fetting out: a draught of new milk
would have been a luxurious banquet to a tired and
thirfty fportfman. On a nearer afpect of this almoft
rooflefs tenement, (its outfide confifting literally of
clay and fticks interwoven together) it feemed more
like a fhed for cattle, to feek refuge under from the
adverfe ftorm, than the habitation of a human being;
but what was my furprize, when on entering, inftead of finding a fhepherd, or a cow-boy, to direct
my weary fteps, ftretched on the bed, (or rather the
floor) of poverty, in a dirty linen garb, lay apparently
in ficknefs, one of the faireft forms of Nature's
work— flaxen ringlets, remarkably long and ftriking,
meandered in difhevelled order, nearly to the bottom of her waift.—The figure of an aged matron,
with her head inclined downwards, and clafping a
delicately white hand, fat forrowing by her fide.
Loft in wild admiration, I had gazed fometime un-
perceived, when Plato bounced paft, and put an end
to my reverie.

Addreffing the old woman, who had juft raifed her
eyes from the ground, I approached, and my conjec-
tures were confirmed.——Death feemed fufpended but
for a few minutes :—— the fair objeƈt of my enquiry
appeared infenfible to what paffed; her countenance
which was engagingly expreffive, pourtrayed the
mixed traits of forrow and hopeful refignation; her
eye-lids half clofed, difplayed long dark lafhes, the
more beautiful from the contraft of light hair, and,
though evidently in extreme illnefs, her cheeks ftill
retained a faint glow which flattered with flender
hopes of life : it was that kind of face which would
at once attraƈt the beholder's admiration; and
though it might not, perhaps, bear pulling to pieces
by the fcrutinizing eye of female envy, yet boafted the
charm of modeft fweetnefs, blended with good-nature,
more pleafing fometimes, than the regular lineaments
of perfeƈt, but often inanimate beauty.

No time was to be loft ; interrogatories and an-
fwers fucceeded each other, and I found from her
guardian nurfe, that MARIA had been feized with
a pulmonary complaint (under which fhe frequently
laboured) three weeks fince, lingering in the ftate
I beheld her, with little relief or affiftance the whole

time; the *Doctor*, to be fure, had fent her fome
draughts, (a few empty phials lay fcattered on the
ledge of a broken window, expofed to the north
wind, which at intervals blew directly upon MARIA's
emaciated frame;) in truth, her little all was expended, and *Sangrado*, in his profeffional purfuits,
obferved one invariable rule: it was his maxim
never to labour in vain.

Gracious Heaven! thought I, and is Beauty's
lovely offspring thus fuffered to perifh, unpitied and
unaffifted?—It was a good three miles to the village where the Doctor lived, but directed to a neigh-
bouring farmer, by the help of a ready faddled fteed,
I difpatched an honeft countryman, who in lefs than
an hour had reached the hamlet, and returned again
with this ragged fon of *Efculapius*, who refembled
much the defcription of Shakfpeare's Apothecary;
but, alas! our efforts were vain.—MARIA had juft
breathed her laft, and lay a clay-cold corpfe. A fe-
rene fmile, the emblem, as it appeared, of happinefs,
fat upon her lifelefs features; lovely even in death.
Moved with the affecting fcene, I gazed in filent forrow, and dropped fome tears upon her Angel form:—
the Doctor's countenance evinced little concern,—
his heart and *Edmund's* were made of different

materials:— perhaps a profeffion which expofed
him often to fimilar fcenes of diftrefs, might have
harden'd his feelings, and rendered them callous to
thofe fenfations which EDMUND felt; and that affliction, which he could not witnefs without par-
ticipating the tender effufions of poor old MARGA-
RET's grief— for fhe fat weeping bitterly by the
bed-fide of her departed friend.—I rewarded this
mock *Phyfician*, (a diftinction he had affumed) for
his trouble, and we parted.

Too much interefted with my adventure, and pre-
vented by humanity abruptly to leave the cottage,
I had now time for reflection; and curiofity as well
as other motives, prompted me to inveftigate the
labyrinth in which I was immured, and to unravel
a myftery, at once fo novel and romantic. I learned
from the good old woman, that fhe had known
MARIA about fix months, previous to which fhe
had lived in the fervice of a widow lady in the neighbourhood; but that on finding the work too hard for
a fickly conftitution, fhe left her place, and had fince
fought a livelihood by making of bafkets, (an art
which fhe herfelf had taught her) and carrying
them for fale about the country; adding, that MARIA
had often told her, fhe was by birth and education

a gentlewoman. That she had written a little history of her life; but, never having been instructed in writing, she knew not what it contained.

I desired her to produce the memorial,— I perused it in tears; and, if I had only wept before, I now felt the pangs of real distress; penned in a style that would have done credit to a performance composed at any age, with the advantage of classical erudition; she enumerated in pathetic language, as far as recollection enabled, the innocent pleasures of her early infancy, advancing in a progressive manner to the period which closed her existence.—The daughter of a country gentleman, and heiress to a considerable fortune, she had received a brilliant education, beloved by her friends, and happy in the affection of a tender parent. Thus had the fleeting years rolled on in peace and gaiety, till that age when the mind begins to expand, and love, often in the garb of friendship, steals, by soft insinuation, its unobstructed passage into the female bosom. Among others who visited at her father's, was a gentleman of small property in the West-Indies, agreeable in his person, and of amiable manners and disposition: attached by mutual inclination, happiness or misery depended on their union or separation; and at length in the

frantic hour of intoxicated love, they eloped, and fet
fail for Barbadoes, where the marriage ceremony was
to be folemnized, but ere they had reached the
anxious port which was to crown all their wifhes,
the being in whofe fate was centered her every
thought, inherited a watery grave: a fatal fhipwreck
had been the confequence, and MARIA, with five
mariners only, (by whofe affiftance fhe had furvived
the ftorm) were the fad remainder of the haplefs
crew; and, but for them, when returning fenfe informed her of her lofs, fhe would have dafhed from
the rock which favored their efcape, and perifhed
with her lover in the devouring deep :— but fhe was
referved for future mifery: left to fcale the fummit
of defpair and wretchednefs, caft on a ftrange fhore,
friendlefs and unknown, and all parental concern
eftranged, fhe became a prey to defpair and want,
which at length rendered her an eafy conqueft to the
wiles of man; but fcarce had fhe culled the glaring
flowers of vice, than withering in her hand, fhe
hurled them from her touch; returned difgufted
from the gaudy path, and fought again, repenting,
the tracks of virtue. Once more landed by her
falfe admirer, (who promifed a fafe paffage) on her
native fhore, hopelefs and forlorn, fhe determined

on the more pleafurable occupations of humble life; for however fweet the rofes with which illufive fancy may deck the ways of vice and diffipation, woeful experience proves that there lurks beneath them many a poifonous thorn; whilft the peaceful avenues which lead to Virtue's facred temple, are ftrewed with evergreens, that flourifh in undecaying and immortal purity. With thefe reflections, fhe wandered from village to village in fearch of employment, and at laft had found, if not a happy, at leaft a calm afylum in the retreat of induftry.

Thus, the unpitied victim of remorfe, fhe had only reached her three-and-twentieth year, when death clofed an exiftence, which could not have been prolonged but in mifery. But for that one irretrievable error, her character was fair and fpotlefs: could that have been effaced, and had it pleafed the Almighty to have reftored her to the world, as *Sterne* thought of *his* MARIA, fo would I have thought of *my* MARIA, and have realized his fentiments.— Yes, MARIA, I would have warmed thee in my own bofom; thou fhouldft have fat at the fame board with me, have fhared the fame repaft, and have been to me perhaps a wife: but fate and heaven ordained it otherwife, and it is well. Wrapt up in sentiment, I left the humble roof which had given birth to the most interesting scene in a yet unexperienced life, and plodded my way in the dusk of evening to my retired cot, fatigued and sorrowful.

My mind entertained not the smallest doubt respecting the truth of MARIA's narrative; and had I been inclined, I wished not to question its veracity. After necessary refreshment, I sought the pillow of repose, and awoke the next morning, as it were from a visionary dream, and scarce able to convince myself, that the scene I had been witness to, was more than the mere illusion of fancy. Alas! it was but too true! the pleasures of the field were for the present only a secondary consideration; my thoughts were more pleasingly engaged: a few guineas made but a small decrease in my finances, and when expended in the cause of humanity, the idea became doubly pleasing. I resolved, therefore, on seeing MARIA decently interred; and ere a week had elapsed, her poor remains, attended by a few village peasants, were borne to their long dark abode, unhonoured by the tear of pity, or the groan of lamentation; but that they might rest in peace, and revive in happiness, was the prayer of EDMUND.

Though, from motives of delicacy, and to avoid the abuse of unmerited scandal, I mixed not in the train at MARIA's funeral, (a task which would have been a gloomy satisfaction to one of my disposition) yet often during my retirement would I visit alone, as it were by stealth, her deserted grave, and strew it with autumnal flowers: my enthusiasm was carried to a romantic height, and the circumstances have left an indelible impression on my memory. On the annual return of that day which gave them birth, I pursue my sport in a kind of pensive pleasing melancholy, intermingled with undescribable sensations of regret and happiness, and sighing repeatedly, as I muse along, alas, MARIA!

(Signed)

EDMUND.

" Ah, little think the gay, licentious, proud,
Whom pleafure, power, and affluence furround;
They, who their thoughtlefs hours in giddy mirth,
And wanton, often cruel, riot wafte;
Ah, little think they, while they dance along,
How many feel, this very moment death,
And all the fad variety of pain:
How many fink in the devouring flood,
Or more devouring flame : how many bleed,
By fhameful variance betwixt man and man :
How many pine in want, and dungeon glooms;
Shut from the common air, and common ufe
Of their own limbs: how many drink the cup
Of baleful grief, or eat the bitter bread
Of mifery: fore pierc'd by wint'ry winds,
How many fhrink into the fordid hut
Of cheerlefs poverty :"   THOMSON.

LETTER

TO THE

EDITOR OF THE TIMES.

(Written during the late fevere Winter.)

Mr. EDITOR,

      THE preceding lines (which
I think fhould be engraved on every perfon's hand-
kerchief, at this time fo frequently coming in con-
tact with the watery eye and the running noftril)

occurring to my recollection, when contemplating the lamentable ftate to which many of my fellow-creatures are reduced by the prefent rigid feafon, have induced me to addrefs you on the fubject of phi-lanthrophy: you are at all times ready, Sir, to ftand forth a Champion in the caufe of the diftreffed, and are daily the defender of your Country, and the bleffings which Englifhmen enjoy.

Generofity has ever been the juft characteriftic of the Britifh Nation, more particularly fince the un-happy revolution in France; and I am glad to find, in your paper of this day, that the Duke of N—TH—BER—ND has fet the laudable example of relieving the neceffitous: but it not unfrequently happens, that thofe who are bleffed with wealth, are lefs fenfible to the fufferings of their inferiors, than others, whofe inclinations would lead them, but whofe circumftances will not permit them, to afford fubftantial relief. Like the Poet therefore, I ad-drefs myfelf, not to thofe whofe hearts are open to charity, but to others, who rolling in immenfe riches, feem to confider their ftarving countrymen an order of beings diftinct from themfelves, and merely born to contribute to their own eafe and confequence: fuch characters there are in this metropolis, and

fuch men deferve the lafh of rebuke.—It appears
contrary to the principles of nature, that avarice
fhould be the vice of old age, but fo it is : the Mifer
tottering upon the brink of the grave, ftill hugs himfelf over his bags of gold, and at the laft hour, when
Death's alarum bell fummonfes him to his dark
abode, his countenance will brighten up from the
reflection of the beloved metal, fo interwoven with
his thoughts.

At this time, no individual whatever, placed
above the ftings of indigence, can be excufed
from contributing his mite towards filling the crav-
ing coffers of the needy. How juft then is cenfure,
when aimed at thofe, whofe fituations enable them
to diftribute univerfal good, and who neglect this
important Chriftian duty. Let them banifh from
their memory the mean proverb, *Charity begins at
home,* and inftead of proftituting their ftately manfions to oftentatious hofpitality, convert them into
temporary afylums for the poor. Let the haughty
Patrician, indulging on the canopy of coftly comfort,
reflect, that many are they who at the fame inftant
are perifhing on the cold ground. Let the fafhion-
able Spendthrift, inftead of carrying his hundreds
to the Pharo Table, vifit the fhed of penury, and

dive into the dungeons of the wretched. The paths
to mifery are not fo intricate but that he may readily
trace the way. A Dutchefs of D—VON——IRE,
when glittering through power and affluence, in the
meridian of beauty, and the Englifh youth flutter-
ing in her train, difdained not to vifit the cottage
of want, and the prifon of the unfortunate. She forgot not her own fpecies, and remembered fhe was
but mortal : her actions evince that fhe conftantly
carries in her fympathetic bofom, the mottos, γνωθι
σιαυτον, *Memento mori :* (know thyfelf, let me remember that I am to die) and reflecting that fhe owed
her envied dignity to mere chance, or that Providence had thus exalted her, in order to difpenfe
good to others, fhe judged it her duty to cheer the
miferable, and to dry up the tear of affliction.
Amiable Senfibility ! lovely Philanthropift ! furrounded by the vanities of a captivating feducing
world, fhe knew how tranfitory was its ftate, and
how empty the word greatnefs, except when attached
to purpofes of benevolence. No oftentation directs
her liberal hand, for her fupplies are generally fecret,
and the wretched object of her compaffion, knows
not from whence the generous portion comes. Such
examples ought to be held up to public admiration.

Let others, endowed with equal means, put on her
God-like nature, and difpatch their private agents
in fearch of wretchednefs.   It is inconfiftent with
the belief of a great and merciful Providence, to
fuppofe, when looking down upon an hundred of
his creatures, that he fhould doom ninety-nine to
mifery, and *one* only to every blefling which the ter-
reftrial world can beftow: he has doubtlefs wifely intended, that *that* one, fo eminently diftinguifhed
from the reft, was for the purpofe of conveying
happinefs to a certain portion of his fellow-creatures ; and Heaven will never countenance fuch vile
perverfion of her gifts as fhe muft daily witnefs.
Ye fons of affluence and oftentation, reflect that
the grave knows no diftinction ; and that the foul,
ftript of its gaudy apparel, and covered only with its
worldly vices, will appear poor indeed, when cited
before the dread tribunal of an impartial Judge, and
an offended Creator.

Thefe reflections, Mr. EDITOR, naturally lead the
Philanthropift to confider the fituation of the Emi-
grant Refugees, towards whom this country has difplayed fuch commendable and unexampled fupport;
and the additional influx of Foreigners, which the
perturbed State of Holland is now daily pouring in

upon us, demands the ferious attention of Government, and of every Englifhman.—Let us ftill continue to imitate the example of the good Samaritan, and pour oil into the wounds of the afflicted; but at the fame time, let us watch at the doors of *Frenchmen*, in order to diftinguifh the *fnake in the grafs*, from thofe, whofe fituations claim commiferation, and pull from the face of the perfidious the mafk of hypocrify. Such men are fuccoured in this capital, and who, fhould their countrymen ever realize their chimerical and phantom-like invafion, will be the firft to re-unite under the crimfon banners of their brother murderers and robbers.—But fear not, Britons! " England," (as Mr. Wyndham obferved in a late debate, in bold and manly language) " has met France fingle-handed in her *proudeft* day."—Let our croaking Jacobins, recall to mind the *Invincible Armada :* let them picture the fleets of Spain, occupying feven miles in length upon the threatening ocean, terrified at the undaunted cliffs of Albion, and beaten from her fhore, the remnant of their colours transfufed with blufhes, returning difmantled, and in fhameful confufion to their own coafts. If ever the boafted determination, *Delenda eft Carthago*, fo often quoted in the Convention, is fulfilled, it

will be by the fons of our own foil. Rome, humble
as fhe now appears, was once the haughty miftrefs
of the world, and what was the caufe of her down-
fall? that laid her temples in afhes, and levelled
her profperity with the duft?—Luxury and Diffipation;— and Luxury and Diffipation are the only
foes of which Britannia need ftand in awe. Let us
prepare for the event, but let the idea of an invafion
vanifh; but fuppofing it accomplifhed, and the
French actually landed upon Englifh ground; the fons
of Albion are ready to rife in arms to protect their
rights, their property, and every thing that is dear
in life: the manufacturer to leave his loom, the huf-
bandman his plough, and the mechanic his trade.
Let the ftandard of CONSTANTINE be raifed in the
middle of our Ifland, and its every inhabitant, me-
tamorphofed into a temporary warrior, furrounded
with rocks and waves, and no hopes remaining, but
in refiftance, will rally round its facred influence at
the trumpet's folemn fhout, in defence of their God,
their Families, their Country, and their King!—
While our fair Chriftian Country-women, with
anxious but undifmayed countenances, their infants
protected within the ramparts of their arms, will
watch at their doors like Spartan Matrons (the ties

of natural affection for a while fufpended) to in-
quire,— not the fate of their hufbands, their fons
or their relatives,— but "if the *Battle's* won?" and
"*with this*," Britons, "ye *fhall conquer ! ! !*"

I am, Sir, yours, &c.

(*Signed*)

A DEFENDER *of the* POOR,

LONDON,
January 21, 1795.

And of my COUNTRY,

⁎ It may be proper to obferve, that the above Letter (being
periodical, and partly of a political nature) was introduced *here*,
in confequence of a particular requeft; but the Author prefumes
no apology will be deemed neceffary by the Reader, from thofe
who efpoufe the caufe of the wretched, at *any time*, or *in any place*.

NOTES and EXPLANATIONS.

Note A.

Adieu to Harrow.—*Line* 14.

" We've painted future blifs o'er Windred's ale."

A Public-houfe famous for good ale.

Note B.

same poem.—*Line* 19.

" And you, *Black Ben,* who oft with threat'ning nod."

Black Ben! a mifnomer applied by the Boys to Dr. H——, the head Mafter.

Note C.

same poem.—*Line* 25.

" My Arnold! fhall I quit, unnotic'd, you?

The Lady with whom the Author boarded; and he here takes an opportunity to acknowledge her kindnefs and protection.

Note D.

SAME POEM.—*Line* 33.

" Adieu, fweet Grove, beneath whofe fpreading fhade."

The Grove belonging to Sir JOHN RUSHOUT's houfe, where the head boys were allowed accefs, and ufed frequently to compofe their verfe exercifes.

Note E.

SAME POEM.—*Line* 37.

" And you, ftern Lion, who with roaring voice."

A Lion is reprefented, and placed on the top of the School, over the Bell, from the Founder's name being Lion.

Note F.

VERSES *on the Ruins of the* PANTHEON.

Line 1, *Stanza* 11.

" Ye made-up groups, no more to vault in air."

The Author here collected the fentiments of JOHN BULL; attended to the fcene of ruin by a fox-hunting companion, who had little relifh for thefe refined amufements; he appeared much delighted at the many imprecations vented by the populace againſt the poor Italians ; and on parting, requeſted me to exerciſe my poetic talents, (ſuch as they were) in lamenting the downfal of ſo noble a building, but at the ſame time by all means to baniſh the Italian race from the ſoil of Britain.

Note G.

SAME POEM.—*Line* 1, *Stanza* 13.

" Quick then, depart from this ill-fated Iſle."

From the ſingular circumſtance of two Opera-houſes being conſumed by fire, in ſo ſhort a ſpace of time; viz. The King's Theatre, and the Pantheon, then uſed as an Opera-houſe.

Note H.

SAME POEM.—*Line* 4, *Stanza* 13.

" But ſecret keep what *ſhame* would bluſh to tell."

Alluding to the immenſe ſalaries laviſhed on Italian performers.

NOTE I.

ELEGY *on the Departure of a Family from a* COUNTRY-HOUSE.—*Line* 1, *Stanza* 2.

" When mufing, *Sedley*, 'mid thy blooming flowers."

Sedley! a fictitious name fubftituted for the real one.

NOTE K.

SAME POEM.—*Line* 2, *Stanza* 2.

" Forgetful Pride appear'd with wand in hand."

Particular circumftances occafioned the writing of this Poem, which cannot be explained to the ftrange reader, (at leaft in a note) and thofe who know the author, are fufficiently acquainted with them.

NOTE L.

SONNET IV.—*Line* 6.

" Ye focial walks within yon facred bow'r."

Sacred Bow'r!—The Grove, facred to the Mufes.

Note M.

SONNET VII.

SAVILLON *taking leave of* ROUBIGNE'S RETREAT:

From the Tale of Julia de Roubigné.

Julia de Roubignè is a well-known Tale, in a feries of Letters, tranflated from the French, and the fingular circumftance which directed them into the hands of the original poffeffor, renders it not improbable, that the ftory they relate is the recital of truth; and there may poffibly have exifted a *Savillon* and a *Julia*, as there did an *Abelard* and an *Eloife*. The following notes are added in explanation of thofe paffages from whence the Sonnets are taken. They who wifh to be more particularly acquainted with Julia de Roubignè, are referred to the ftory in toto: it will pleafe fuch as delight in the perufal of a mournful tale, and who blufh not, in condefcending occafionally to vifit the regions of romantic woe. It differs from the common run of thofe productions, entitled Novels, in which is generally found a mixture of good and bad, high and low character. *Here* the characters are all noble, the fentiments refined, and the language penfively beautiful.

Savillon and Julia were the children of two friends. Savillon's father had been unfortunate, and Julia's parent had been the friend of his misfortunes : they had never told their love, but the eyes, thofe faithful indicators of a virtuous paffion, had expreffed it in more forcible language than the tongue could have done : ignorant of that period when love ceafed to be the love of children, and friendfhip grew into paffion ; Savillon's departure, (whofe deftiny drives him from his native country) firft revealed to them their fatal attachment; with a beating heart he leaves the coaft of France, in fearch of that wealth, which he valued only, that it might render him the more worthy of Julia. While abroad, a falfe report prevails of Savillon's marriage, which induces Julia, in obedience to parental wifhes, to accept the hand of Count Louis de Montauban, the friend and benefactor of her father Pierre de Roubignè, but her heart knows no other than Savillon ; and from thefe unhappy nuptials iffues the melancholy fequel.

NOTE N.

SONNET VII.—*Line 5.*

" Th' untrodden glade, to love and virtue dear!"

" In the receffes of Roubignè's retreat, there was a wild and rocky dell, where taftelefs wealth had never warred on nature, nor even elegance refined or embellifhed her beauties. The walks were only worn by the tread of the fhepherds, and the banks only fmoothed by the feeding of their flocks : *there*, too dangerous fociety ! did Savillon pafs whole days with Julia : there, more dangerous ftill ! did he pafs whole days in thinking of her."—See *Julia de Roubignè.*

NOTE O.

SONNET VIII.

JULIA *watering the Flowers, which* SAVILLON *had planted, with her Tears.*

" The day previous to Savillon's departure for Martinique, while taking an evening walk about the grounds, and examining fome curious feeds, put into his hand by Roubignè, he dropped a few on a fpot called Julia's garden. Not long after he was gone the flowers appeared: Julia would frequently fteal unobferved to watch the growth of thofe flowers, and when they began to droop, fhe watered them with her tears."—See *Julia de Roubignè.*

NOTE P.

SONNET X.—*Line* 4.

" And haggard Poverty prepares a tomb."

" Savillon had few friends, and he feemed not to wifh them many, (fuch, however, as the world commonly call friends) Beauvaris, who ranked among the number of thofe few, was the brother of his foul, and his latter days faw him ftruggling with Poverty." See *Julia de Roubignè.*

NOTE Q.

SONNET XIII.

MONTAUBAN *meditating the Death of his Wife* JULIA.

Montauban believing his wife to have difhonored the marriage bed, meditates her murder: the circumftances which led him to fuppofe her guilty, are fufficiently ftrong to difturb the quiet of a jealous and haughty mind.—Savillon's concealed picture is difcovered wet with Julia's tears.—She breathes his name in her fleep, accompanied with deep fighs, confents to a private meeting, &c. and Montauban thence banifhing from his thoughts every idea of her innocence, adminifters poifon.

NOTE R.

SONNET XIV.

Julia, in her laſt letter to Maria, after having imbibed the fatal potion, predicts her approaching end : recalls over the paſt ſcenes of their early lives, and bids a long farewell to her amiable and virtuous friend.

NOTE S.

SAVILLON *at the Tomb of* JULIA.

We hear nothing further of Savillon, after having taken his laſt leave of Julia : but it is no great ſtretch of fancy for a Poet, eſpecially when writing from romantic events (nor even ſhould there really have exiſted a Savillon) to picture him at the tomb of his departed lover : ſituated as the tale relates him, it is perfectly compatible with the feelings of nature, to imagine on his receiving the tidings of Julia's untimely end, that the paſt ſcenes of their fateful lives, would ruſh with freſh vigour upon his tortured mind, and that he would trace out the ſpot where her remains were depoſited, in a ſtate of melancholy diſtraction.

Note T.

Tributary Lines on the Arrival of the MARQUIS CORNWALLIS *from* INDIA.—*Line* 13.

" When (fafe on board) the parting Swallow heav'd a figh."

The Packet in which his Lordfhip came paffenger to England.

Note V.

EPITAPH *on a* FARMER.

Some time elapfed, before the perfon on whom this Epitaph was written, difcovered the author of it, and when informed, that it was from the pen of one, whom he had feen grow up from an infant, the good old man became deprived of utterance, and " fhone in tears."

Note U.

VERSES *on a Church-yard, at* MOON-LIGHT.

Line 4, *Stanza* 7.

" Here fall his honors, and here dies his name."

Although his name may live on the monument from felf vanity, or the pride of relatives, it graces not, perhaps, the page of hiftory, and by his country is remembered no more.

Note W.

SOLAR ECLIPSE.—*Line* 2, *Stanza* 2.

" Fair Virtue's Enfign view'd the train."

An Horfe acted as Enfign in bearing the Colours to the Camp.

Note X.

ADIEU TO COLLEGE.—*Line* 34.

" Nor longer, now, the tutor, fage divine !
" My bills will ftretch, or praife my London wine."

Poets are allowed the privilege of fiction, and fhould thefe lines ever meet the eye of the author's learned and refpected tutor, he hopes he will not cenfure him for having made ufe of that liberty in its full extent: but where is the philofopher fo ftrictly confcientious, and fo dead to the bleffings of independence, who, tranfplanted from a bed of thiftles, and placed for a few moments in a garden of fmiling rofes, that will not be tempted to fip their fragrance.

ere the rude wind and the fleeting feafon, diffipate and deftroy their fweets.

Note Y.

SAME POEM.—*Line* 37.

" The prying Proctor, too, the mean-earn'd fee,
" No more fhall force to prove his poverty."

There are certain fines exacted by the Proctors, when they find the ftudents without bands, or any other part of their academical appendages; by which privilege, fhould they be inclined, they may reap a plentiful harveft during their Proctorfhip.

Note Z.

SAME POEM.—*Line* 41.

" And thou, fam'd Frank, with cheeks of crimfon hue."

Frank Smith, the Mafter of a celebrated Coffeehoufe at Cambridge, called the Union; and diftinguifhed for his genuine humour and a red face.

DIRECTIONS

FOR

PLACING THE PLATES.

Let each Plate (except the **Frontifpiece**) **face the Poem it reprefents, viz.**

Plate   I. (the Frontifpiece) **to face**   **The Title** Page.

——   II. **to face** the Poem, **entitled, Stanzas on** hearing the Screech-Owl.

—— III. **to face** .... Elegy written on **the** Sea Coaft at Margate.

—— IV. **to face** .... Savillon at **the Tomb** of Julia.

——   V. **to face** .... **Stanzas** on a Church-yard.

—— VI. **to face** .... **The Fragment.**

ERRATA.

Page 1 Line 13 of Introduction, *for* mead, *read* meed
—— 14 —— 3 Stanza laſt, *for* ſhrieks, *read* ſhriek
—— 36 —— 13 *for* bluſt'ring, *read* bluſhing
—— 47 —— 2 *for* magic, *read* dazzling
—— 53 —— 7 *for* eer *read* ere
—— 57 —— 3 Stanza IV. *for* hate, *read* hated
—— 62 —— 5 Stanza III. *for* loaths, *read* loathes
—— 71 —— 3 *for* beech, *read* beach
—— 73 —— 12 *for* e'er, *read* ere
—— 85 —— 3 Stanza III. *for* preſs, *read* ſtamp
—— ib. —— 2 *for* drafts, *read* draughts
—— 92 —— 13 *for* ſwallow, *read* Swallow.